SOMETHING TO HOLD

SOMETHING TO HOLD

Katherine Schlick Noe

CLARION BOOKS

HOUGHTON MIFFLIN HARCOURT

BOSTON • NEW YORK • 2011

⫷⫷═◉═⊨⫸⫸

Clarion Books

215 Park Avenue South, New York, New York 10003

Clarion Books is an imprint of
Houghton Mifflin Harcourt Publishing Company.

www.hmhbooks.com

The text was set in 13-point Norlik.

Map by Jennifer Thermes

Library of Congress Cataloging-in-Publication Data

Noe, Katherine L. Schlick (Katherine Logan Schlick)
Something to hold / by Katherine Schlick Noe.
p. cm.
Summary: In the early 1960s, Kitty is one of only two white children in her class on
Warm Springs Reservation, Oregon, where her father is a government forester, and
although past injustices and pain are still very much alive there, she eventually finds
friendships and opportunities to make a difference. Includes map, author's note,
glossary, and pronunciation guide.
ISBN 978-0-547-55813-4
[1. Race relations—Fiction. 2. Family life—Oregon—Fiction. 3. Schools—Fiction.
4. Indians of North America—Oregon—Fiction. 5. Forests and forestry—Fiction.
6. Warm Springs Indian Reservation (Or.)—Fiction. 7. Oregon—History—20th
century—Fiction.] I. Title.
PZ7.N67178Som 2011
[Fic]—dc22
2011009639

Manufactured in the United States of America
DOC 10 9 8 7 6 5 4 3 2 1
4500326551

For Louella,
who took a stand

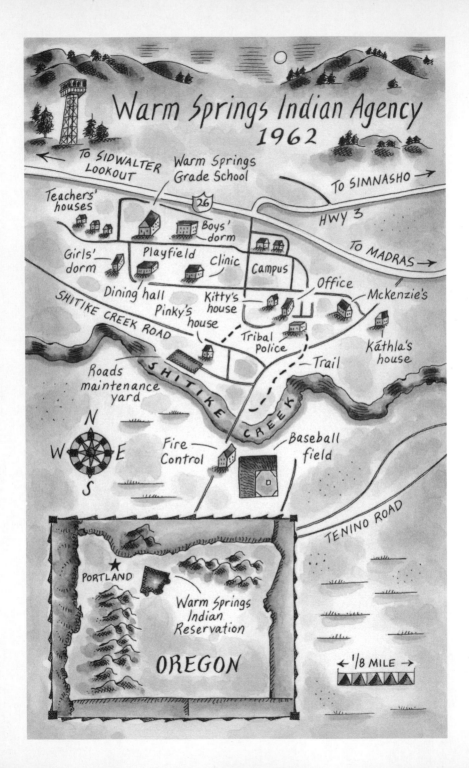

Báshtan

AUGUST 1962

STATION One, this is Sidwalter Lookout. *Come in!*" A woman's voice, strained and urgent, drags me out of sleep.

Seconds later, the siren on the roof of the jail across the alley goes off, so loud it hurts. Something's wrong.

I know what's coming next. A door clicks open in the hallway, and suddenly, light seeps through the crack under my door. Then my dad's bare feet cut a shadow out of the strip of light.

"This is Station One. Go ahead, Sidwalter." He is talking into the two-way radio, and he is calm, like always.

The woman comes back on.

"We've got lightning strikes on the other side of

HeHe," she says. "I can see the glow from here." I recognize her voice. She checks in every night from the fire lookout tower way out in the woods. August is danger season for forest fires.

"Ten-four," my dad confirms. "Keep an eye on it. I'm headed down to Fire Control and will call you from there. Station One out."

Dad doesn't move. He must be staring at the map of the Warm Springs Reservation taped to the wall. He'll be tracing the web of lines anchored by Mount Jefferson at the corner of the reservation and by the rest of the Oregon Cascades. Looking for water sources and access roads. Getting his mind all the way awake and focused on fire.

Steps echo again in the hall, heavy this time: Dad's fire boots. The rusty spring on the back door creaks open.

Next, I hear the pickup start, back away from the garage, and turn in a sharp spray of gravel. And then the night is still again.

I wish I could go back to sleep, but my heart is racing and my mind is showing me pictures of fire. I breathe slowly and let my thoughts drift.

Funny, I know the Indian women up on the fire lookouts—Mrs. Wesley on Sidwalter Butte, Mrs. Quempts on Shitike, Mrs. Suppah on Eagle—better than any of the kids who live at Warm Springs. My brothers have already made friends. A guy named Jimmy showed up the day we moved in and asked them to go to baseball practice. Now Jimmy comes around just about every day and they go off somewhere, leaving me a sitting duck when Mom wants chores done, which is almost always.

We've been here two weeks, and I haven't seen even one girl.

⟨⟨⟨HOH⟩⟩⟩

In the morning, I follow voices out onto the windowed porch. Mom is bent over the sewing machine, making curtains. She looks perfectly comfortable, as usual, despite the heat.

Bill is standing in the doorway, peeling his damp T-shirt away from his chest.

"How are you going to get there?" Mom asks, like she always does. I wonder where he wants to go.

"We can walk. It's not that far."

She sighs, then holds up a hem and cuts the thread with her teeth.

"Mom, we'll watch out for cars," Bill says. "We'll be fine. Please?"

Finally, she nods. "OK, but you have to be extra careful." She always says that, too.

"Great. Thanks, Mom!"

I follow Bill into the kitchen. "Where are you going?"

Bill reaches into the cereal box and takes a handful of corn flakes, which he crams into his mouth. "Swimming," he says, chewing. "At the creek."

I know about the swimming hole in the cold, fast-flowing creek up Shitike Road. We've driven to it, but for some reason Mom doesn't want us to walk up the road. In Virginia, we could walk anywhere.

I'd give anything to splash around in the water. "Can I go?"

"Just Joe and me with Jimmy," Bill says.

I hate when he makes me beg. "But...I want to come."

Bill shakes his head. "Find your own friends."

Easy for you to say. All the kids here are boys. I pour the last of the cereal into a bowl.

Mom comes into the kitchen. After a small silence, Bill huffs and says, "*C'mon,* Mom."

She is staring him down. "Bill," she says, "Kitty goes—or nobody goes."

I can't believe she's taking my side! I spoon up my cereal fast, in case she changes her mind.

Jimmy is waiting on the back steps. The four of us scuff up the alley and then leave the shade of the big trees for the open and dusty trail that winds down the hill to Shitike Road. It's scorching out, but the crushing heat feels bearable now that I'm headed for cold water.

The road is quiet, just a cluster of houses and a couple of dogs panting in thin shade behind a fence. I don't know any of the Indian families that live down here.

The pavement ends, and the rest of Shitike Road stretches out in front, a dry graveled ribbon all the way to the mountains. Bill and Jimmy walk ahead, talking baseball. Boring stuff, like how 1962 is a great year because some guy named Jackie Robinson got elected to the Hall of Fame.

Jimmy's the catcher for the VFW Little League team. Any boy at Warm Springs can join, even Joe, though he hasn't played yet. Bill's on third base, but his heart is set on pitching. Yesterday he came home all happy because the regular pitcher got benched. Maybe he'll get his chance tonight. It's the last game of the season.

I drop back, keeping out of the dust that they kick up. Joe trails behind, flinging gravel into the ditch. Walking to the swimming hole takes much longer than going by car. Finally, we come to a straight stretch where I can hear the creek tumbling off to the left through the thick brush.

Bill and Jimmy stop and look back.

"Remember where the trail is?" Bill calls.

Trees and bushes press close on both sides, coated with dust. I don't see any trail. "I don't think this is the right place."

And then something blasts past my legs, skitters through the gravel, and plunks Jimmy right in the ankle. A rock the size of my fist.

"*Ow!*" he yells, and crumples into the dirt.

Bill whirls around to look back at Joe. "What the heck are you doing?"

But Joe didn't throw that rock. He's way behind us, standing in the ditch to one side of the road. A wedge of Indian kids in cutoffs and shorts comes up behind him, a tall girl in the lead. And she looks really mad. "Hey, *Báshtan!*" she shouts.

"What's that?" I ask Bill. He shakes his head.

Jimmy straightens up, brushes the gravel from his legs. "What do you want, Jewel?" he calls.

"You know her?" Bill asks, surprise in his voice.

"Oh yeah." Jimmy nods. "*Everybody* knows her."

Now a boy pushes through the group and steps out in front of the girl named Jewel. On his feet are ragged tennis shoes. He holds a rock in his fist.

"Uh-oh," Jimmy says quietly. "Raymond."

"Who's that?" I ask.

Bill sighs. "Trouble."

The Pitcher

THE boy named Raymond is as tall as Jewel and looks just as angry. He flips the rock up and down in his hand and says something I can't hear. Joe's head jerks away, his arm comes up. Raymond raises his fist.

Joe's only eight. Raymond towers over him. *"Hey!"* I yell.

"Kitty!" Bill says through his teeth. "Shut *up*."

Raymond turns and stares at us. Then he lets the rock fly. I duck behind Bill and cover my head as the rock skips through the gravel and lands in the ditch.

Raymond waves his hand off toward the creek. "This is our spot," he says. His voice is hard and angry. "You don't belong here." He points up the road. "Go on that way."

The Indian kids disappear through the brush.

I'm so angry — or maybe scared — I'm shaking.

None of us wants to stay and argue. We take off and get a good hundred yards farther before I can make myself stop and turn around. The road behind us is empty.

"Who *is* that kid?" I ask.

"The pitcher who swore at the coach yesterday," says Jimmy. "Again."

He bends down and touches his ankle — a big old goose egg, swollen and purple.

"So, you get to pitch tonight?" I ask Bill.

"Yeah," he says. "That rock was probably meant for me."

I want to get off this stretch of open road and away from those angry kids. "I don't want to go swimming anymore."

"*C'mon,*" Bill says. "They're gone. We'll find the path up here and forget about it." But he just stands there, not going any farther.

Finally, Jimmy says, "Aw, let's go home." He turns away from the sun and limps down the road.

Bill shakes his head at me and Joe. "Not a word to Mom," he says. No worry about that — she'd never let us go anywhere again if she knew.

I'm sweaty and dusty and scared. I don't see any of the Indian kids, but I can hear them shrieking and laughing in the water. We start the long walk back toward Warm Springs.

At the curve at the end of the straight stretch, Bill calls, "Car!" and waves us off into the ditch. For once I'm glad he's here to order us around. I didn't even hear the engine.

I turn to see a roiling cloud of dust and gravel and then a battered black pickup bearing down on us. It skids to a stop just ahead and slowly backs up.

"Now what?" says Jimmy.

The pickup pulls alongside us and stops. The driver leans out the open window—an older Indian woman about my grandma's age. "What're you kids doing out here?" she asks. She has a deep blue scarf tied over her hair, and her face is creased deep, stern. I can't see her eyes behind her dark glasses.

There is a pause. Bill points back up the road. "We were going swimming."

"Your folks know?"

Jimmy nods quickly and so does Bill.

Then she peers down at Jimmy's ankle. "Looks like trouble."

Jimmy and Bill nod again.

"Back there," the lady tilts her head, "is the swinging bridge. That's the Indian kids' swimming hole. Yours is about a half mile farther on."

"Yeah," says Bill. "We found out."

She kind of chuckles, then says, "Long walk on a hot day. I'll give you kids a ride home."

I don't want to walk anymore. Mom will have a fit if we take a ride with a stranger, but this lady is nice.

"No, thank you," Bill says. "We're fine."

I'm disappointed. We're never allowed to ride in the back of Dad's truck, since it's for official use only. And way too dangerous, Mom says. I notice Jimmy's ankle. It's purple and huge, and blood is dribbling down into his tennis shoe. We need to do something.

"A ride would be great," I say quickly. "Thank you."

Bill shakes his head at me, but I ignore him. "We live on the upper campus, right by the office," I tell the lady.

She nods. "Your dad's the new forest manager."

How does she know? I wonder as we scramble up into the bed of the truck, and she takes off down the long road.

<<<<HOH>>>>

When we pull into the driveway, Mom is out in the yard watering the zinnias. She frowns when she sees us in the back of the pickup. We spill out of the truck bed as fast as we can.

As the lady comes around the front of the pickup, Mom sets down the hose and walks over. "Oh, hello," she says, smiling and extending her hand. "I'm Mary Schlick."

The lady takes it and smiles up at her. "My name is Bessie," she says. "I found your children out on Shitike Road."

She's wearing a cotton dress that goes down to the tops of the moccasins on her feet. The dress is navy blue and tied at her waist with a woven belt. An underdress in pink calico, tight at her wrists, shows under the wide sleeves draping over her shoulders. Mom told me it's called a wing dress. When we first got here, I noticed that most of the older Indian women who go into the tribal offices next to our house wear them.

Jimmy hustles around the side of the house, forcing himself not to limp. I know better than to catch Mom's eye, but Joe looks up.

"Honey?" she asks. "How was the swim?"

"Great, Mom, good time, gotta go to the bathroom." And he jumps for the steps and slams the back door.

Bill and I hang back. I wonder if the lady is going to tell Mom the whole story about how we met.

"Would you like to come in for a cup of coffee?" Mom asks.

The lady smiles and shakes her head. "Gotta get to McKenzie's for the mail." She climbs back into the pickup.

"Thank you for the ride," I say, relieved that she didn't tell Mom anything else.

I hurry through the house to my bedroom, sniffing for the hint of smoke that clings to Dad's clothes after a fire. There's nothing in the air. He hasn't come home yet.

My bedroom window is open, shaded by the big locust tree. As I change back into shorts and a T-shirt, I hear Mom talking in the yard.

"You *promised* me." She does not sound happy.

"We stuck together," Bill says, his voice calm.

"How come you didn't swim?" she asks.

"What?"

The toilet flushes, and Joe opens the bathroom door. I wave him into my room. "Listen to this."

Mom says, "...and nobody's hair was wet."

"It was a long walk. Before she picked us up."

"And what happened to Jimmy's ankle?" she asks.

Bill stalls. "We didn't want to tell you this, Mom..." he begins.

Gee — don't just give it to her!

"...but Joe was throwing rocks."

Joe sucks in a big breath. I clamp my hand onto his arm and glare at him. *Keep quiet.* He looks like he is about to pop.

I can hear Mom's sigh all the way in here. "Did he apologize?"

"Oh, sure. Jimmy wasn't sore...well, he *was* sore, but it's not going to hurt his catching or anything."

Joe gets the whole *What were you thinking?* lecture. I'm surprised that he takes it. But he scowls at Bill: *You owe me.*

That's What You Think

MOM shoos Joe out of the house. "Go find a friend and stay out of trouble," she says. Then she points to Bill. "You come with me."

Bill rolls his eyes but follows her out to the porch. I grab a book and join them, for the company.

Mom's working on a new shirt for his first day of junior high. Now she makes him stand while she fits the sleeve, pins sticking out of her mouth. I sprawl on the padded bench under the porch windows and ignore his insulted groans.

After a while, the back door slams and steps pound up to the kitchen. "Mom?" Joe yells from the other side of the house. Then he appears on the porch, dusty and sweaty. "Guess what?"

Bill twists around, and Mom grabs for his arm before he can wrench the sleeve away. "Hold still!"

"Howie Granger and me have Miss Tutwiler," Joe says. "We went up to the school and saw the class lists."

"Howie and I," Mom says automatically. She pulls the pinned-up shirt off Bill's arm.

Who's Howie? I wonder as Joe leans against the doorway. *And how come he can find friends when I can't?*

"You've got some guy named Nute," Joe tells me.

"Newt?" I ask. "You mean, like a lizard?"

"No, like N-u-t-e. What kind of name is that?"

Mom lines up the seam and stitches the shirt together as Bill disappears off the porch, pulling Joe with him.

Class lists tacked up on the school door. My stomach hurts at the thought of starting all over.

Mom meets my eye. "Remember how it was in Virginia when we moved from the apartment into the house? You had to go to a new school in the middle of third grade, and you fit right in."

"That was different."

"How so?"

I'm not sure how to explain how I feel. Finally, I say, "I've never gone to school with Indian kids."

"Kitty, you knew lots of Indian kids when we lived on the Colville Reservation," Mom says.

"I was a baby. That was a million years ago. Way before we moved to Virginia."

She smiles. "You just have to get to know these kids."

"They won't know why we're living here and going to their school."

Mom puts her hand on my shoulder. "Honey, *everybody* on the reservation knows why we're here. Because your dad works for the government. Just like the other non-Indian families."

I think about Jewel and Raymond and the rock out on Shitike Road.

"Why can't we go to school in town?" I ask. *Where most of the kids are white.*

Mom clips the thread and holds up Bill's shirt. It looks like something right out of the Sears catalogue. She folds it, sets it on her lap, and looks at me. "Because your school is here," she says, like that answers everything.

We would have blended in up there in Madras. But I don't say this out loud. Mom takes the shirt into the living room, giving my head a gentle pat as she goes by.

⟨⟨⟨‖O‖⟩⟩⟩

Before supper, I sit in the shade on the back step and watch for Dad's pickup. Mom calls from the kitchen, "Honey, go find the boys. We've got to eat so they can get down to the game."

"Will Dad be home in time?" Bill asks when he comes up the steps into the kitchen.

Mom plops mayonnaise into a bowl of potato salad. "Hope so," she says. "Now that school's about to start, fire season should be winding down."

I wish she wouldn't talk about school. Those mean kids will not be happy to see us there.

"What does *Báshtan* mean?" I ask.

Mom sets down the spoon. I should have kept my mouth shut.

"Where'd you hear that?" she asks.

"Somebody said it."

"Who?"

"A girl." I know that won't be enough, so I take a breath and give up the rest. "Out on Shitike Road, by the swimming hole."

Mom frowns at Bill. "There *is* more to the ankle story, isn't there?"

He nods slowly.

"Why don't you tell me what really happened," she says.

And he does.

I wait for the storm. But Mom says only, "How come you didn't say that in the first place?"

He opens his mouth and the truth pops out. "'Cause

we thought you'd never let us go there by ourselves again."

"So you decided to *lie* to me?" Mom shakes her head and gets up to clear the table.

Bill is grounded. His pitching season is over before it even starts. I feel kind of sorry for him, but Joe has "paid in full" smeared all over his face like butter from popcorn.

I finish up the dishes while Mom helps Joe look for his glove. I don't know why he needs it; he just sits on the bench. She comes back into the kitchen as I swipe the sponge across the table, scooping crumbs into my hand.

"I didn't answer your question," she says.

"Yeah. *Báshtan.*"

"It means 'white person.' Not in a nice way."

The room is now shadowed by evening. "Why did she yell at us?" I ask. "We just wanted to cool off in the water."

Mom holds up the wastebasket so I can shake off the crumbs. "I know, honey." She is quiet for a moment. "So that's why you want to go to school in Madras," she says. "You'd feel comfortable there, with more white kids?"

I nod, relieved that she said it, not me.

Mom doesn't look mad, just thoughtful. "You know

your dad's work is very important," she says, "to him and to the tribes. That's why we've chosen to live here. I know it's hard being new, but people are kind and generous here. If you give that girl a chance to know you, you'll see."

I work hard to keep the tears out of my voice. "I don't want to be here," I say. "I want to go home."

Mom puts her warm hand on my shoulder. "Kiddo," she says gently, "we *are* home. And someday soon it's going to feel like it."

Maybe she does understand a little bit.

She gives me a hug. "You know how to make friends," she says to the top of my head.

Joe clomps back up the stairs, his glove in hand. "We gotta go."

Mom looks at his sneakers. "Tie those things before you break something," she says. "Then Kitty will take you to the game."

"*What?*" I stare at her. "I can't go by myself."

"I have to stay here in case Dad calls in," Mom says. "And Joe will be with you. It will be fine."

That's what you think.

⊰⊰⊰◄◄◄∘►►►⊱⊱⊱

The game is all the way down at the ball fields on the other side of Shitike Creek. We hurry down the alley past the jail, where a tribal policeman is pulling something

· 19 ·

out of the trunk of his patrol car. He slams the lid and calls out to Joe, "Hey there, squirt."

"Hi, Mr. Wewa!"

"You boys play hard tonight. That team from Crooked River is tough."

Joe waves his glove, and Mr. Wewa takes his gear into the building.

"How do you know *him?*" I ask. Joe's quick to make friends, I know, but this guy is a grownup—and a policeman.

Joe shrugs his shoulders like it's obvious. "This is the way we go to baseball. He always asks me how I'm doing. He's nice."

Joe leads me to the trail that winds down the hill to the baseball field. When we get close to the backstop, he sprints ahead, and I'm on my own.

I don't know anybody in the stands. And it seems like everybody is staring at me. I climb to a spot at the edge of the bleachers, close to home plate. From here, I can look around without feeling quite so awkward.

Our side of the bleachers, along the third-base line, is filling up. So is the visitors' side, between home and first. The team we're playing is from a little town off the reservation. Over there, it's a sea of white faces.

Jimmy is crouching behind home plate, taking

warm-up pitches from one of the players. His ankle is bandaged, but he's putting weight on it.

The coach, Sherf, walks up to Joe at the end of the bench. "Where's your brother? We need him on the mound."

Joe shrugs. "At home. Grounded."

Sherf shakes his head. No pitcher, no game. He goes over to talk to the umpire.

A car pulls up behind home plate and stops with the bumper almost touching the backstop. The driver has his cap pulled down low. He says something over his shoulder to two kids in the back. Then Raymond slides out of the passenger side, followed by that girl, Jewel.

Oh boy. I wish I'd picked a spot in the middle of the fans. I slouch down, hoping they won't notice me.

Raymond stands beside the car, checking out the field. Then his face settles into that scowl I saw out on Shitike Road, and he walks right up to Sherf. "I'm here to play," he says.

The coach thinks about this for a moment before handing Raymond a glove. "Get in there, then."

Everybody stands for the flag salute. Our coach holds his VFW cap across his chest and the players do the same. With the last words, "With liberty and justice for all," something makes me glance down from the bleachers. Jewel stands beside the car, staring hard at me.

⋘ ⋙

When we walk up the alley after the game, the kitchen light is on. The green government pickup is parked in the driveway. Fire boots on the back step. Dad's home.

He is standing at the kitchen sink when we come in. "Hey, I'm sorry I missed your game," he says, lifting Joe's baseball cap off his head. He has changed out of his fire clothes, but I can still smell them. He looks tired.

Dad scoops me into a hug. "We whipped that fire into shape in no time flat. You knew we would," he says.

I'm happy to see him. For this moment in his warm arms, I'm not worried about making friends. But it won't last long.

Howie

SUMMER turns the last corner and runs head-on into the long school year. Suddenly I'm sitting at the kitchen table in a new school dress, picking at pancakes.

Joe is on his third helping. All the dirt from the last few weeks has been scrubbed off his face, and his summer crew cut has grown out a bit. He splashes half a bottle of syrup onto his plate. If Bill doesn't hurry up, there won't be anything left. Mom leans into the back hall and calls down to the basement.

The stomping on the stairs sounds different, not like the soft thump of summer sneakers. Bill stops in the doorway to let us admire him. His new side-tie shoes are slick with polish, and white socks peek out from beneath his pegged pants. The new shirt fits him perfectly, like he's some teen idol in stupid glasses.

"Nice threads," Dad says, reaching for bacon.

Bill jabs a pancake off the plate before his bottom hits the chair. "Gotta get going," he says. "Jimmy's saving me a *good* seat on the bus."

Mom hands him a glass of milk and says, "Take it easy. Don't slop breakfast all over my handiwork."

The first-day-of-school routine is different this year because we won't all be together. Bill will abandon us for a long bus ride that climbs out of the canyon to the junior high in Madras. Joe and I will carry our new tablets a few blocks to Warm Springs Grade School. Makes me want to throw up.

"Honey?" I realize Dad's talking to me. "You want me to walk you to school this morning?"

Joe shakes his head before I can get my mouth open. "You don't need to come."

Yes, you do! I finish off my orange juice instead of saying so. Too embarrassing to have your dad take you to school in the sixth grade, no matter how much you need him.

"OK. I've got a timber meeting in Prineville, but I'll be back before dinner. You can tell me all about it then."

Mom checks the clock over the stove. "Bill, scoot!" She shoos him with her hands, and we all scatter in different directions.

All the way across the campus, I think about what is

ahead. When we get to the stop sign by the basketball court, I see a thread of students climbing up over the lip of the hill from Shitike Road. Indian kids. Joe and I are the only white kids, and even with our brown hair and summer tans, we stick out.

The school is flanked by two dormitories — for girls on one side and boys on the other. Not long ago, this was a boarding school just for Indian kids. Last year, the Bureau of Indian Affairs turned the school over to the county. Now everybody in grade school comes here. Some Indian kids stay in the dorms if their homes are way out on the reservation.

My throat gets tighter when I see the mass of kids around the stone steps of the school building. Not a grownup in sight.

"I'm going to go find Howie," Joe says.

"*What?* No—" I blurt, but he takes off toward the playground, leaving me exposed on the sidewalk.

I take a deep breath and tell myself, *Today's the first day of school everywhere. All you have to do is look for somebody standing all alone, smiling. Better yet, somebody scared spitless. Go say hi. Simple as that.*

A pack of girls pushes out through the doors of the dormitory across the way. Then the door of the boys' dorm bursts open behind me, and I'm caught in a swirl of black-haired kids. Not one of them looks half as scared as I feel.

I grip my tablet and work my way to the edge of the crowd. That's when I see a white kid about my age standing off to the side of the playfield. There's something odd about him, like his face wasn't put together right. Plaid shirt buttoned up all the way and tucked into his pants, belt cinched tight. He has a big grin plastered on his face. I walk over, and I'm about to say something when Joe trots up. "Hey, Howie. I was looking for you."

Howie points at him. "Joe," he says to me.

"Yeah, I know. I'm his sister."

Joe looks around at the crowd. "Lotta kids here, huh."

Howie nods. "Huh."

What's with this kid? I look over at Joe. "I thought you said you and Howie are in the same class."

"We are," Joe says. "He's my friend."

But he's older than you. And what's wrong with him? I can't ask this in front of Howie, so I smile and say, "Oh. Nice to meet you."

Howie glances over my shoulder, and the grin disappears. I turn to see Jewel and another girl slice through the mob. The other girl stops right in front of me, her feet bare in scuffed white flats, like she's trying to look cool. Jewel stands beside her, watching. I hold my breath, trying not to flinch.

"Looks like the *re*-tard found some company," the girl says.

I wish I could disappear.

Howie's shoulders sag. "That's not nice, Norma," he says.

I'm stunned. How can that girl be so mean? I can't think of a thing to say.

Joe tugs on his sleeve. "C'mon, Howie. Let's go." My little brother has the nerve to stare back at Norma. He and Howie push through the crowd of kids that has gathered around us.

Norma smirks, turning back to me. "Friends of yours?"

Jewel hasn't said a thing this whole time, but I can feel her eyes on me.

I don't know where it comes from, but I'm not scared anymore. I'm mad. "Yeah," I say. "And you leave them alone."

I turn away, cross the street, and start up the steps to the front door. A bell suddenly begins to clang, and the students of Warm Springs Grade School surge into the building.

Good German Name

THE main hallway is a cavern. A tall man stands inside the door, nodding over the crowd like he's counting heads. This must be Mr. Shanahan, the principal.

He spots me. "You're new," he says, like I might not know.

"Uh-huh."

I'm supposed to go to the office to check in. Mr. Shanahan steps into the traffic to create a narrow opening, and I slip through it into the office. It is quiet in here, just a lady standing on the other side of the counter filling out a form. The other students must already know where they belong.

"My mom called last week?" I say when she doesn't look up. "To register us?" I have no idea where Joe is.

He's supposed to be in here with me. I run my hand nervously through my short hair.

"Oh, right," the lady says. She sets down her pen and pulls a file card out of a box in front of her. "Kitty and Joe Schlick?" I nod. "You're in sixth grade with Mr. Nute. Your brother is in third with Miss Tutwiler." She looks behind me. "Where is he?"

I sigh and shrug my shoulders. The lady smiles slightly. "We'll find him, make sure he gets to the right place. You go on to class now."

When I come out of the office, it's hard to see with so many kids pushing through the hall. Mr. Shanahan says, "Down there," and points to a classroom straight ahead where two hallways meet.

Just above the crowd, I see a bald head standing sentry outside the door. This must be Mr. Nute. I go with the tidal wave of kids right into the classroom.

Inside, the desks are bolted to the shiny wood floors. Straight rows all facing front. A name card written in ragged script is taped to each smooth, slanted desk. We have assigned seats. I hope mine is by the windows, out of the way.

Jewel stands at the first desk in that last row. She's staring at me. Suddenly, I'm not as sure of myself as I was a few minutes ago.

"You," she calls across the room, and points to a desk about halfway down the next row.

A boy whirls around when she speaks. He is short and skinny, and his shirt is pulled out of his pants. He peers down at the name card on the desk. *"Kitty,"* he says, smirking. "Here kitty, kitty!" Then he laughs like an idiot.

Oh, geez. It seems like the whole room freezes, everybody turned toward me. In that spray of faces, only one other is as light as mine—a kid who looks like a bozo with a blond crew cut and black-rimmed glasses. I quickly slide past Jewel and into the seat.

"Shut up, Orin," she says to the skinny kid.

One of the boys grins and pokes Orin on the arm. "She told *you.*" And the pack turns and chews on one of its own.

I just can't figure this Jewel out. I concentrate on the smooth plane of my desk. Then something catches my eye. Raymond stands in the doorway. His steady eyes hold mine for the instant before I look away.

Another bell rings and Mr. Nute pivots into the classroom, pulling the door shut behind him. Everyone scatters and sits.

Mr. Nute spends a minute writing on the board, his name appearing in chalk in the same slanty print as on our name cards. Then he turns to face us, hands clasped behind his back like a soldier at ease. There is a weird symmetry to the way his stomach mirrors the shape of his bald head. His pants are cut wide to fit around him, and they sag over shined cowboy boots.

"Good morning, class," Mr. Nute says. "Welcome to sixth grade."

Reading from his clipboard, he calls the roll. Albert, Brunoe, Charley. Then a pause. "Cull-piss," he says.

The boy beside me snorts and then slaps his hand over his mouth. Giggles ripple across the rows, but no hand goes up.

Mr. Nute repeats himself, this time scanning the class. "Here or not?"

A girl in the next row throws a look over her shoulder. "Orin—that's *you!*" she hisses. Orin slowly raises his hand.

"Tomorrow," Mr. Nute says, "answer me the first time." He traces his finger down the list. "Dan-zuck—"

"Excuse me," Jewel says, rising from her desk.

Mr. Nute looks up, brow creased.

"His name is Orin Culpus."

"That's what I said. *Cull-piss.*"

"No," she replies, her voice calm and clear. "It's Culpus."

Mr. Nute looks at her for a long moment, then back down at his list. "Dan-zuck-uh."

"*Danzooka.*" Jewel blends the syllables in three graceful beats. "Here," she says, and sits back down.

Shaking his head, Mr. Nute makes a mark and then repeats, correctly this time, "Danzuka."

Slouched down in his seat, Raymond lifts his hand a couple of inches off the desk, index finger up. Mr. Nute scans the room before he sees it.

"Say 'here,'" Mr. Nute says.

"I'm here."

Are Raymond and Jewel related to each other?

Mr. Nute makes his way through a whole string—Franklin (the kid with the blond crew cut), Kishwalk, Moses, Polk. All the hands go up.

He takes another glance at the list, another pause. "Shil-ick."

I hate having a name that nobody can pronounce. I sigh and raise my hand. Every year I have to do this.

"It's Schlick."

Mr. Nute nods. "Good German name," he says.

<hr/>

At recess, I stand at the edge of the field. In Virginia, I could join any group on the playground and feel welcome. But not here. Not after this morning.

A crowd presses around the backstop of the baseball diamond. I go over there so I don't feel so stupid out in the open. Nobody moves over to make room for me right by the fence, so I stand a little bit behind the other kids. The only thing to do is act like I don't care.

Raymond leans over first base, razzing the batter, a kid named Benson whose desk is next to mine. Jewel stands on the mound, ready to pitch. She and Raymond look like they might be brother and sister. I wonder why they're in the same class.

Jewel hurls the ball, and Benson swings hard and misses for the third time. "You're out!" yells Raymond, and Benson tosses the bat and jogs off toward the outfield.

They're playing work-up. You start in left field, and with every out you work your way up until you bat. Jewel trots over to the backstop to join the batters, and the fielders all rotate.

Raymond moves over to the mound as Franklin, the other white kid in my class, wags the bat over his shoulder. He crowds home plate, a wide grin on his freckled face.

Raymond wipes it right off with his first pitch. He rears back and fires a pitch that hits the batter square on the arm. Franklin howls, twisting away. The bat flies out of his hands and lands in the grass. "Stay off the plate!" Raymond hollers as Franklin drags himself to first, folded up around his elbow.

The boys who are waiting to bat all shrink away from the plate. Jewel steps around them and shakes her head, disgusted. She picks up the bat and holds it over her shoulder. Calm and cool, she stares back at Raymond.

Something passes between them. I can't read it, but all the kids stand still. Then Raymond winds up as the recess bell clangs. He throws a bullet straight toward home.

Jewel hammers it — out over the players, the street, and the playground beyond. The ball clears the fence, bounces once on the highway, and vanishes into the tumbleweeds on the far side.

Jewel stands on the plate glowering at Raymond. "You don't throw at the batters," she says, and turns back toward the school, carting the bat with her.

Wow. Where'd she get the nerve to do that?

⪻⪻◅◄◉►▻⪼⪼

After school, Joe is waiting for me in front of the building, like Mom told him to. I shake my head. "Where were you this morning? We were supposed to go to the office first."

Snapping at him doesn't make me feel any better. I'm actually proud of him for sticking up for Howie.

"Howie took me to class," Joe says. "Miss Tutwiler let me sit behind him."

As we head for home, he fills the air with his nonstop talking, and for once I'm grateful for his chatter. This feels normal—like the old days when we walked down the hill from our school in Virginia.

At supper, Dad acts normal too. "So, how did it go?"

Bill jumps right in, rattling on about how cool it is to change classes every hour. This gives me a few minutes to sort through my day. Mr. Nute taking roll seems better than all the other embarrassments I could tell them about.

When I get to the part about Jewel correcting him, Dad shakes his head.

"There was a Danzuka on the tribal council a few years back," he says. "This is the girl from down at the creek?"

"Yeah."

"If she's from the same family, she's been raised to speak up."

I'm not sure what he means. Jewel didn't speak up when Norma called Howie a retard. She just stood there.

But she told Orin to shut up when he made fun of

my name. And she corrected Mr. Nute. She even stood up to Raymond on the baseball field.

After helping with the dishes, I settle in at the dining room table with the spelling list Mr. Nute had scribbled across the board. *I have to go back tomorrow. And it'll be as bad as today.*

My throat feels tight, and the words on the paper are blurred by my tears.

Bill tosses his algebra book onto the table across from me. He pulls a pencil out of his back pocket and sits down. "What's wrong with you?" he says.

I shake my head, wiping my dripping nose with the back of my hand.

"You're *crying?* About *homework?*"

"Shut up." I keep my head down, sniffling the tears back in.

Bill opens his book, flips through a few pages, and starts in on the problems. I sit there like a big dope, my face all wet and slobbery, until he says, "*Geez*—here," and hands me a wadded-up tissue from his pocket.

I take it—I don't care where it's been.

"It'll get better, you know," he says.

"Yeah?" I sniff. "When?"

Bill scribbles numbers across the page. "When you make some friends."

"You sound like Mom."

He smiles, puts down his pencil. "Sometimes she's right."

I blow my nose on his tissue. "Thanks."

"You're welcome," Bill says, and we finish our homework together.

It's a Start

ON my first Friday morning at this school, I stand off to the side of the playfield, waiting for the school doors to open. This has become my usual spot, though it always feels a little exposed. I watch out for Jewel and Norma. Then I notice the empty swings along the fence separating the field from the girls' dorm. That may be a better place to wait.

I thread a path through the little kids playing tag and am almost to the swings when I see Jewel and Norma sitting on the grass. They lean back against the chainlink, and Norma is holding one hand down in the grass. I get a weird feeling about this, but it's too late to turn back.

Norma lifts her chin. "What're *you* doing here?"

I could kick myself for walking into this mess. But

I'm not going to show it. "Just came for a swing." I keep my voice as even as I can.

Norma shakes her head. "They're taken."

"There's nobody here," I say.

"I didn't say that." She shrugs. "Just said they're reserved."

Norma checks the field for a second, then lifts up her hand and puts it to her lips. *She's smoking!* One quick puff, and she hides the cigarette back down in the tall grass. She stares at me. "You gonna tell?" she asks.

Like on the first day of school, Jewel doesn't say a thing.

"Course not." I turn around and walk away.

⋘◄◦►⋙

Franklin is leaning against the front-step railing joking with Benson as I come up to the school. The nasty bruise Raymond gave him shows under the sleeve of Franklin's T-shirt, but he grins at me, so maybe it doesn't hurt that much.

"How's it going, new girl?" Benson asks.

I've had it and am not in any mood to be teased or picked on. His face looks friendly, though.

I sigh. "I hate being new."

"I know what you mean," Franklin says.

"Your dad work for the Bureau of Indian Affairs too?"

Franklin chuckles. "Worse—Presbyterian church.

I'm a preacher's kid, and we've moved all over. Getting started is hard everywhere."

This is the longest conversation I've had in weeks. It feels so normal, so good.

I nod toward the bruise. "Did Raymond do that because you're white?"

"You kidding?" Benson says. "Take a look at half the boys in this school. Raymond does stuff like that 'cause he *can*. He doesn't care who you are."

The first bell jangles above our heads, and Benson heads for the front door. Franklin picks up his books, then turns back to me.

"Look," he says, "you gotta start somewhere. Just... jump in. You'll be surprised."

And he jogs on up the stairs and through the doors.

I walk into the classroom and almost bump into a girl standing just inside who's got a group gathered around her. I've never seen her before, and for an instant, my hopes lift. *Maybe she's brand new, like me.*

The girl turns, and I realize that I can see over her head. She is tiny and has long, black hair held back from her face by red barrettes. Suddenly, I feel tall and clumsy.

A girl named Geraldine slips around the jam we've created in the doorway and grins when she sees her.

"Hey, Pinky. It's about time you got home. How was the summer up on the lookout?"

Pinky rolls her eyes. "*So* boring. I thought I'd be stuck on Sidwalter Butte forever."

In my mind, I hear the voice from the two-way radio outside my room: *"Station One, this is Sidwalter."* The voice that watches over the woods for fires and keeps me company while I sleep.

"You got to stay up at the lookout?" I ask. I'm envious. The radio makes it sound so exciting.

Pinky sighs like this is a bad thing. "We left the day after school got out and came down last night." She gets a puzzled look. "You're new. How do you know about Sidwalter?"

This is the first time I've known about *anything* since we moved here. "I can hear Mrs. Wesley on the radio. You had a big lightning storm a week or so ago."

"Yep," Pinky says. "That's my mom."

"And Station One is my dad."

Pinky's eyebrows shoot up. "Oh, I know about you," she says. "You just moved here from back east."

I nod. "Yeah."

Pinky suddenly shouts out to the kids milling around the room. "Hey, you guys!"

Every head turns. I shrink back against the doorway, wishing I was invisible.

Pinky points her elbow at me. "She's OK."

I feel my face begin to glow. *What is she doing?*

"They think you're stuck up."

I am too surprised to say anything. I try not to think about all the kids who are now staring at me.

"Geraldine says you haven't talked to anybody. You don't smile."

My heart is pounding, and I'm about to lose it completely. *This is so unfair!*

But Pinky smiles. "I knew that wasn't true. Mom said she really likes working for your dad. And she said I'd like you, too."

I swallow hard, locking the hurt inside. Then I breathe in and try to smile back at her. "I'm glad you told me," I say, finally. "I had no idea."

The final bell rings and Mr. Nute walks through the door. As everyone scrambles to their seats, Franklin gives me a quick thumbs-up.

My desk is down the row from Geraldine's. I make myself look at her.

"Hi."

Geraldine stares at me for a second. Then she says hi back.

Franklin is right. It's a start.

Not Like That

ON Sundays we drive out of the canyon and up to the church in Madras. Going to church feels normal and familiar, no matter where we live.

I'm nervous but hopeful as we head up the highway, just like I've been every week. The kids in Sunday school see each other every day in school, and we're the only family that drives in from the reservation. Still, fitting in here, where all the kids are white, feels like it's going to be easier than at school.

My parents go straight to the sanctuary, and Bill heads upstairs with the junior highs. I follow Joe to Sunday school in the basement. Joe peels off into his classroom, and I hesitate for a second at the doorway of the sixth grade room.

It would be so great if someone would wave to me.

Come sit by me — there's a seat over here! But nobody says a word.

Cathy Watson is sitting on the far side of the room. As usual, all the chairs around her are filled with followers. Cathy is the kind of girl teachers trust with notes to the principal, the kind born to be prom queen. That first Sunday, she made a point of saying hi and introducing me to a few of the girls. That was nice, even though they all went roller-skating after church and I went home to Warm Springs.

A couple of kids bump past me as the teacher, Cathy's mom, shoos us away from the door and over to the chairs. Mrs. Watson picks up her Bible, and I drop into the first empty seat.

I'm trying to be subtle about wiping my sweaty hands on my dress when a girl next to me swings around in her seat, her blond ponytail almost hitting me. A new girl. As she moves, her stiff petticoat rustles.

She says the worst thing right away. "I was saving that seat."

I can feel my face get hot. "Oh — sorry."

"For Cathy," she says, like I should know.

I try to sound confident and casual. "She's sitting way over there. She won't mind."

"Maybe not," the new girl says. "But I do."

We stand to sing "Onward, Christian Soldiers," and

the petticoat takes up most of the space between us. I have to lean sideways toward the pudgy boy beside me, which makes him tip closer to the next kid. And so on. A whole side of the room tilting to the left. When we sit back down, the new girl folds her hands over her lap to keep her skirt in place.

We are let loose from Sunday school just as the grownups are moving into the coffee room upstairs. I'm standing by the photos of past ministers, cookie in one hand, punch in the other, when Cathy comes up with the new girl. "This is Linda," she says to me. "She just moved here from Bend. She's in my class and Campfire Girls."

Linda holds her cookie like it is a teacup, pinkie raised. "How come I've never seen you before?" she asks.

"Oh, Kitty doesn't go to school with us," Cathy answers for me. "She lives at Warm Springs. You know, the Indian reservation."

"You're Indian?" Linda looks at me kind of sideways.

"No. My dad's a forester. He works for the government. So we live on the reservation."

"You live with Indians? You go to school with them?" she asks.

"Yeah." *What's she getting at?*

Linda shakes her head, arms folded. "We have Indians in Bend. All they do is drink beer down by the river."

I suck in my breath. *What a mean, rotten thing to say!*

"*I* sure wouldn't want to go to school with them," she goes on.

I look over at Cathy. She just stands there smiling in her sweet way. Maybe she didn't hear.

More of the girls who orbit around her have bubbled up. "My uncle has to follow them around his store to make sure they don't steal anything," says a chubby girl whose name is Karen. A bite of cookie bulges inside her cheeks.

"And remember when that kid pulled a knife on my brother out behind the high school? They're all like that." This is from Nadine, who has red hair. Her dress is a bit short, and it is tight across her chest where her boobs might be someday.

I thought that Jewel and Norma were mean, but in their own way these girls in their nice Sunday clothes are just the same. They cluster around Cathy. As more girls appear, Linda slowly edges me out. Pretty soon, I'm looking over her shoulder into the circle.

"See ya," she says. And she gets them all moving around to the other side of the punch table, and I'm left standing at the wall.

Cathy smiles back at me and waves goodbye. Linda

leans in at her elbow and whispers to her, then the pod moves off down the hall.

Bill appears, a stack of cookies in his hand. "Mom and Dad ready to go yet? And who's that blond girl?"

"She's new," I say.

He chews as he watches the procession disappear. "So, what's the matter?" he asks.

"Nothing."

Bill leans back, his right foot flat against the wall holding him up. His casual pose.

"Do you hear kids talk about Indians?" I ask him.

"What do you mean?"

"Well, do they say things about drunks?"

"Some," Bill says. "Why? What'd those girls say?"

"That Indians are drunks and steal stuff."

He holds a cookie ready to pop into his mouth. "And what did *you* say?"

"Nothing. I couldn't think."

"You should've said something. That's stupid." I think he means them, not me. Somehow, I feel a little bit better.

"Well, I didn't. They don't care what I think." Except for Cathy, who must not have heard what Linda said.

<hr>

We usually stop at the store for something on the way home from church. Mom doesn't believe in passing up an opportunity. Sunday dinner gets put off even longer while we pick up bananas or canned milk for my dad's coffee.

We drive just until the highway pulls up the hill out of Madras, and we stop at Erickson's. I go in with Mom while Dad and the boys keep the engine running and listen to the radio. We split up to save time. I go to find bananas that are still a little bit green, and there are Cathy and Mrs. Watson in the produce aisle, picking out Brussels sprouts.

Mrs. Watson sees me first and smiles. "I sure appreciated how attentive you were today," she says.

"Thanks."

She checks her list, which is written on the back of a check deposit slip. Just like my mom. "Cathy, I'm going to get the flour. Would you find a nice squash?"

She hurries off, and Cathy rolls her eyes. "Squash— yuck!"

I nod my head. I happen to like baked squash, but it feels good to agree with her.

"Isn't Linda nice?" she asks, picking through the mixed bin. She reaches underneath a couple of bulging butternuts to come up with a tiny, shriveled acorn.

"Well…" I'm not sure what to say.

"She's got a transistor radio," Cathy says, putting

the squash in a paper sack. "We listen to KRCO Platter Party when we walk home from school."

Wow. My parents don't think I need a radio. You can't pick up much from down in the canyon at Warm Springs, anyway. But you can get KRCO out of Prineville, and the junior high kids call in to dedicate songs to each other. Bill says it's how a girl tells a boy she likes him. Not that it's ever happened to him.

"That's neat," I say. Cathy Watson could be a friend. I want her to like me, to keep talking to me.

"You bet," Cathy says.

I take a chance. "I thought that what she said about Indians was mean."

"What? Back at church? Oh, that." She dismisses it with a toss of her curls. "You can't help where you live."

"That's not what I meant." I should keep my mouth shut, but I can't. "Do you think all Indians are drunks?"

"Frankly"—Cathy shrugs—"I don't think about them at all."

That's what bothers me.

⫷⫷⦿⫸⫸

After we eat ham and green beans and I help with the cleanup, I retreat to my bedroom, my favorite place. I take off my dress, find some pants and a sweatshirt. I'm thinking about those girls with their stiff petticoats that poof out their skirts, their hair neatly curled. And how much I don't fit in after all.

There is a knock at the back door. Our house is small enough that through the wall I can hear Mom go down the short steps from the kitchen and open the door. "You must be Pinky," she says, a smile in her voice. "Nice to meet you. Kitty's in her room. Go through the kitchen and keep turning left."

A few seconds later, the door opens, and Pinky sticks her head in. "Barbies?"

"Sure!"

I told Pinky at school last week about my Barbie dolls—a blond with a silky ponytail and a bubble-cut brunette. I only have a few outfits besides the swimsuits my Barbies came in. She likes the tiny shoes best. Last Christmas, I got a hundred pairs stapled into a cellophane packet.

In no time, we have shoes and clothes spread all over my rug, and Pinky is working the blond Barbie into her evening gown.

"What was it like going to school in Madras?" I ask her after a while. "Before they opened up the boarding school?"

Pinky wraps a fake-fur stole around Barbie's shoulders. "What do you mean?"

"Well, were there any other Indian kids up there?"

I wonder if this will feel too personal to her, but something tells me Pinky won't mind.

"Oh, yeah. A bunch of us." She plucks a pair of pink shoes from the pile on the rug and slips them onto the doll's feet.

"Did you know Cathy Watson?" I ask.

Pinky nods. "Sure—she was in my class. How come?"

"She was in Sunday school today," I say. "And some girl with her said"—I hesitate—"something about Indians."

Pinky shrugs and shakes her head. "That we're drunks?" I must look surprised, because she adds, "White people say that all the time."

"I'm white," I say.

Pinky smiles. "Not like that."

She holds up Barbie. Sparkly black evening dress with furs, open-toed shoes showing off red nail polish on her tiny feet.

"Movie premiere," Pinky says. "Hollywood."

We both giggle, and it feels good to laugh with her.

Hail to Thee, Land of Heroes

RIGHT after lunch, Mr. Nute slams down the windows to shut out the highway noise and the afternoon sun. "To help you concentrate," he says. It's October, but by two thirty the room is steaming.

We're rehearsing for the Columbus Day assembly next week. Each class will perform something about America. We're doing the Oregon state song, which is about free men who conquered the Golden West. We've built a rickety covered wagon out of a packing crate and canvas. Now we're stuck learning the words, and we haven't even tried the singing part.

From his desk at the front, Mr. Nute signals Deland to start over.

Deland takes a deep breath and plunges in. "Landatheempirebuilders..."

"*Stop!* It's '*Land . . . of . . .* the *Em*-pire *Buil*-ders.'" Mr. Nute taps out the beat on his desk with a ruler.

Deland stands there in the aisle, clutching the song-book.

"Again." Mr. Nute raises his arms, the ruler now a baton.

"Landa —"

Mr. Nute slams the ruler down on the desk. "*Land OF!*" he blasts. "Good grief!"

Deland flinches and drops the book. We clamp our mouths shut, hold still. The storm will blow over if we don't move.

"Sit."

Deland sits. Reaching down, he scoops up the book.

Mr. Nute scans the rows. He pauses for a second at Raymond, who's hunkered down low at his desk, then nods to Franklin. "Next line."

Each kid reads just one. I don't have to pay attention, because I've counted and there aren't enough lines left.

Franklin slouches at his desk, fumbling with the pages. *He wasn't even following along.* He draws his fist up to his mouth and mumbles into it.

"For Pete's sake, speak up!" Mr. Nute stands, frowning at Franklin, who keeps his own eyes glued to the page. Exasperation rolls in a wave from the front of the room.

"*People,*" Mr. Nute says, "this is our state song. A majestic tribute to every person who came to this land seeking a better life. It deserves more respect."

He sighs again and sits back down. "Orin. Go on."

Orin holds the book up in front of his face like a shield. "Hell to thee..." he reads.

"*Mis-ter Culpus!*" Mr. Nute jumps up, slamming the book on his desk.

Orin looks confused. "What'd I do?"

Mr. Nute stares him down. "It's *hail* to thee," he spits, and points straight out the door. Orin has the good sense to set down the book and go.

Mr. Nute watches to make sure Orin gets to Mr. Shanahan's office. Then he settles himself into the creaky old chair at his desk. "Who's next?" he asks.

This is not a safe moment to raise a hand. In the weeks we've been in school, I've learned to read Mr. Nute. At times like this, it's best to stay out of range.

But it doesn't work. He gets up, walks slowly down the aisle, and stops right above my desk.

"Kitty," he says, "you read the rest for us."

I stand, wipe my sweaty hand on my skirt, and hold the book still so that I can see the words. I read the second stanza and then sit.

Mr. Nute walks to the front of the room, then turns and stands, hands clasped behind his back.

"Kitty," he says, "what is this song about?"

"Explorers," I say.

He rocks back on the heels of his cowboy boots. *"And?"*

I hate when teachers want you to guess what's in their head. "Uh…pioneers coming to Oregon?"

"And *why* are they coming to Oregon?"

I feel like an idiot. But he's waiting. I say the first thing that pops into my head. "This is the land of the free and the home of the brave."

Beside me, Benson snickers and shakes his head. *I know it was stupid.*

That must have been close enough. Mr. Nute says, "OK. At least one of you has some idea what we're talking about."

He starts pacing up the row, boot heels clicking against the polished floor.

"We are *all* immigrants," he says, "And America is the *greatest* country in the history of mankind. It was established on the backs of those who came before us."

Mr. Nute pauses for a second to let that sink in, then he unleashes an oration on Columbus Day and the ideals on which this country was founded. All made possible, Mr. Nute tells us, because this one man and a bunch of others who came after him had the courage and vision to seek out this empty and savage New

World, to plant their flags so that civilized men could tame it, men like our country's forefathers and the great explorers who made the Oregon Territory safe for the pioneers, all of whom sacrificed so much so that we can have the freedom—the unearned and unappreciated *luxury*—to sit here and wallow in our ignorance.

"Now, let's take it from the top," Mr. Nute says quietly. "One more time."

⋘◄◄═══►►⋙

After supper, I have to help Bill drag the garbage can out to the alley. It is already mostly dark now. No more long evenings bathed in twilight.

He holds the screen door open. "Hurry up!" he calls over his shoulder. "I've gotta get over to Jimmy's to finish up our social studies project."

I pull my jacket off the hook in the back hall and follow him. "Something for Columbus Day?" I ask.

"Nah, current events—that thing with Cuba." He bends and twists the garage handle, pulls on the heavy door, and heaves it up so it slides across the metal track above our heads.

"We're having an assembly about Columbus. Every class has to present something on America."

His smile pities me, a kid who has to do such dumb stuff. "And what are you guys doing?" he asks as we wrestle the stinking mess out to the alley.

"The state song. You know, 'Conquered and held by free men.'"

Bill chuckles. "Ironic, huh?"

"What?"

Bill wipes his grimy hands on his jeans. "Well, don't you think it's weird to make Indian kids celebrate Columbus —*and* the empire builders?"

"He discovered America," I say, "and they settled it."

Bill rolls his eyes. "Oh, please," he says. "Think about that."

And he turns and jogs back into the house.

When the Animals Were People

"HAIL…to thee…Land…of…Pro-mise," Deland reads. We have worked all the way back to him.

I think about the long lines of wagon trains and the people who rode or walked all that way across the country. And the seasick masses of immigrants who were drawn to the beacon of the Statue of Liberty from all the way across the ocean. That's how all my ancestors got here, as far back as the pilgrims on the Mayflower. For three hundred years, my genes have stretched across the Atlantic Ocean.

Then it hits me. *This song is about white people.* I scan the room and count—just me, Mr. Nute, and Franklin, who is sitting over there slouched down with his book propped up in front of his face and his eyes closed. *What about everybody else?*

Benson catches me looking around. "What are you doing?" he whispers.

Mr. Nute is way up front, his boots crossed on his desk. So I lean toward the aisle. "Where'd you come from?"

"Huh?"

"Before now. Where are you from?"

Benson shakes his head. "Highway Three," he says.

I take a quick glance at Mr. Nute, then try again. "I mean your family."

Benson shakes his head like I'm not making any sense. "No place," he says. "We've always been here."

"No—I mean *way* back."

I should have quit sooner.

"*Miss* Schlick!" Mr. Nute is standing up, glaring. "Do you have something important to share with the class?"

Nothing to do but look sorry and hope for the best. "No, sir."

He gives his head a little shake. "I expect better from you."

◄◄◄❖❖►►►

Pinky catches me in the hall on the way to recess. "What was that all about?"

It is getting chilly outside. I button up my sweater and shake my head. "Nothing."

She chuckles. "You've hardly said anything in class, and today he's *disappointed?*"

We push out through the big front doors. "Benson says he's always been here," I say.

Pinky turns at the bottom of the steps. "Yeah?"

I try to explain. "Well, everybody comes from somewhere." Kids swirl around us in the sunshine.

For a second she has that same look: *What are you talking about?* Then she says, "Three tribes were put on this reservation. I'm Wasco—we lived up on the Columbia River. The Paiutes were dragged off the desert. But Benson's people are Warm Springs. They were—" she sweeps her arms around— *"right here."*

"For how long?"

"Well—*forever.*" Then Pinky adds, as if it's going to help, "Since the animals were people." And she runs off to play foursquare.

<hr />

When I go into the house for lunch, the kitchen is empty—the table is not even set. I hear soft voices from the living room. Mom sits on a chair pulled up close to the couch. She is handing a cup to an Indian woman about my grandma's age who is sitting back against the ivy pillow. A dark scarf is tied back around her head, and she wears a plaid wool jacket over her wing dress and high moccasins.

Mom says, "Kitty, you remember Mrs. Queah-pama? She gave you a ride last summer."

The woman eases the saucer down onto the coffee table, then reaches out a small, wrinkled hand to me. I quickly cross the floor and take her warm palm in mine. She was wearing dark glasses last time, but when I look into her eyes, I remember her.

"I was resting on your steps, and your mom invited me in for a cup of coffee," Mrs. Queahpama says, a web of smile lines spreading out from her eyes. "It's a long walk from the clinic back to my house."

I smile back and settle myself into a chair by the sofa.

"I've been telling your mom about the old days," Mrs. Queahpama says.

"Very old?" I ask.

"Oh, yeah. When the mountains were young." And then she chuckles and her whole body jiggles.

This is what I want to know. "Were the animals really people once?"

Mrs. Queahpama nods, smiling. "You *are* talking about old times."

"Well, how could they be people?" I ask. I hope I'm not being rude.

Mrs. Queahpama doesn't look offended. "The Creator put our people here," she says, "to care for the land so the Earth will provide a home for all living things. Before people, the animals were the caretakers. My *káthla* and my aunties, when they told stories, they always started that way, 'When the animals were people.'"

"That must be a long time ago," I say.

"Our home has always been here," Mrs. Queahpama says. "Since long ago, when the animals prepared the world for us."

I think about the empire builders. "But then the white people came," I say. "And made Indians live on the reservation."

Mrs. Queahpama leans back into the sofa cushions. "Do you know what that means?" she asks.

I thought I did—that the government made the people live in a certain place. The way she asks it makes me wonder. So I shake my head.

"We signed a treaty with the United States government," Mrs. Queahpama says. "They took almost everything. But we reserved this land for ourselves."

I hear both sadness and pride in her voice.

"Most of us were forced to leave our homes." She nods, then leans toward me. "But we carry our roots with us"—she touches her creased palm to her chest—"right here. So we never forget who we are."

I have to hurry out the door to get back to school in time. The trees haven't shed their leaves yet, all gold and green around the campus. The walk is quiet and sunny, a good time for thinking.

I have no idea how it would feel to carry those roots inside so they'd stay with me wherever I went. I wish I did.

I do know one thing, though. Mr. Nute has never heard of the animals who were people.

A Lot to Learn

MR. Nute hangs his jacket on the hook, picks up the songbook, and stands at the front of the room. It's now or never. I raise my hand.

He looks surprised. "Yes?"

"Mr. Nute...um...I'm wondering about the song."

"Yes," he says again, slowly.

I glance around the room. Everyone else is looking down.

"Well...we're talking about what makes America great—courage and vision and stuff..." This sounds dumb, but I place my hands on my desk to steady myself and keep going. "I'm wondering how it fits."

"We're proud of our state song," he says.

I nod. "But, Mr. Nute"—I flail around for a way to put this—"it's about you and me and Franklin..."

Franklin's head jerks up. He shoots me a look that says, *Why are you dragging me into this?*

I've got to spit it out. "The song's *only* about us."

"What are you talking about?" Mr. Nute asks. And then his eyes narrow. "Stand up if you have something to say to me."

I stand slowly, holding on to the back of my chair to keep my knees from shaking. Across the room, Jewel turns in her seat. Her face flat, she holds my gaze. Then she frowns and shakes her head quickly. The message is clear: *Leave it alone.* The image of Mrs. Queahpama tapping her chest pops into my head.

Jewel rises up from her desk. Mr. Nute swivels his head and narrows his eyes at her. "What about the courage," she says, looking around the room, "of the people who were already here?"

I am stunned that Jewel is standing up for me. She just said exactly what was on my mind, what I couldn't find the words to express.

Red is spreading up Mr. Nute's neck and all over his bald head. When he speaks, his voice is tight. "I have *never* had a student question my teaching," he says.

I get a sinking feeling.

Mr. Nute breathes in deep. His eyes slice the air between us. "Go wait for me in Mr. Shanahan's office."

I can barely breathe, and blood pounds in my ears.

There is no movement anywhere, as if all the kids have melted away. Leaving everything in my desk, I walk up the aisle and follow Jewel's sweater down the hall.

Mrs. Wyatt looks up when we come through the office door. "Yes?"

Then she looks past Jewel and sees my face. "What's wrong, honey?"

I stand in front of her desk like a big goof, unable to respond. I'm in shock. I've never talked back to a teacher or been sent to the principal. Jewel waits silently beside me.

"Mr. Nute sent us to see Mr. Shanahan," I finally tell her.

"You?" she asks. She frowns over at Jewel.

Mr. Shanahan opens the inner door to his office.

"Trouble down the hall," Mrs. Wyatt tells him, tipping her head toward Jewel.

They think she did something, I realize.

Mr. Shanahan holds the door open and says to me, "Come on in. Let's see what's the matter."

He closes the door and motions me toward one of the two big wooden chairs in front of his desk. "Why don't you tell me what happened," he says gently, sitting down in his chair.

"It's not Jewel," I say. "She was just sticking up for me."

His eyebrows go up. "Really? What is it, then?"

Mr. Shanahan sits with his elbows on the arms of his chair, his legs crossed. He's so calm that I stop feeling ashamed and just tell him — about the song, Columbus Day, the animals who were people.

"I didn't mean to be rude," I say at the end. "I just had some questions."

Mr. Shanahan nods for me to go on.

"Mr. Nute said we're all immigrants, but that's not true."

He leans forward. "Did you say that to Mr. Nute?"

"Well, Jewel kind of did." I talk to my hands. "That's what made him so mad."

Mr. Shanahan chuckles, and I look up. His face is serious but his eyes aren't. "You think your class should read something different?" he asks.

I shrug. "I think I should have kept my mouth shut."

Mr. Shanahan smiles. "Well, it's obvious that you meant no disrespect. You understand that Mr. Nute is the teacher, and it's up to him to determine the curriculum." He pauses, and I nod. "So I don't see any need for punishment."

Then he adds, "I expect you to apologize to Mr. Nute, of course."

I nod. I knew that was coming.

I leave his office and sit down by Mrs. Wyatt's desk

while Mr. Shanahan talks to Jewel. When she comes back out a few minutes later, her face hasn't changed. Still closed off and blank.

Mr. Shanahan opens the office door for us. "You'd better get on back to class now," he says, and we slip under his arm and through the doorway.

The hall is empty and quiet. Jewel starts toward Mr. Nute's room, then stops and turns around. "You've got a lot to learn," she says, shaking her head.

"About what?"

"Did you think Mr. Nute would *care* what you had to say?"

"Well, yeah . . . I hoped so."

"He doesn't know the first thing about us." Jewel shakes her head again. "Some people aren't worth the effort."

"So why did you speak up?"

For a second, Jewel stands there. Then she sighs. "'Cause you were making a mess of it," she says. "But you were right."

When the last bell rings and all the kids hurry outside, I walk up to Mr. Nute's desk. He sits with his head down, grading papers.

"I'm sorry."

"Uh-huh," he says. He doesn't look up, just keeps

slashing red pen across the long division problems in front of him. I'm not sure if that means I can go or if I'm supposed to say something else.

After a moment, Mr. Nute sets down the pen and frowns at me. "You want my advice?" It's not a question. "Stay away from her."

"Jewel?"

He nods. "She is going nowhere. None of them are."

How can he say that about his students? Mr. Nute sounds like those girls in Sunday school.

My heart pounds in my throat, but my mouth goes ahead on its own. "If you feel that way," I ask quietly, "why are you here?"

Mr. Nute shakes his head, his eyes frowning. "It's a job." He turns back to the papers on his desk. "They will drag you down if you let them."

Mr. Nute picks up the pen again, and I am dismissed.

Good Riddance, Báshtan

HOWIE leans his nose into the backstop, his fingers hooked into the thick wire mesh. In the student tide that spreads over the playfield between the dining hall and the school, Howie anchors himself in his own little radioactive zone and watches every pitch.

My brother is the only kid who'll stand beside him. Joe doesn't even seem to notice the gap between them and everybody else. He and Howie chat away, watching the game. I'm hoping they don't yell something stupid when I have to bat.

It's the first time I've tried to play. Pinky kept bugging me to get in the game. She says it's the way to make friends in this school. I'm not sure I believe her. I saw what happened to Franklin that first day. But I finally got up the nerve and ran out into left field, even without a glove.

And now I've worked my way all the way up to the backstop. I'm having fun, and so I make sure to keep away from Raymond, who will bat in front of me. I don't want to give him any reason to pick on me, so I slide a few steps away from Howie and Joe.

Benson goes up to the plate and wags the bat at his shoulder. "Babe Ruth looks for his six hundredth home run," he chatters at Jewel, who is on the mound. Jewel winds up and pitches. Benson crushes the ball past third.

"Go!" shouts Howie. Like all the words off his tongue, this comes out kind of thick. The kids standing around the backstop snicker, but Howie doesn't seem to hear them.

Benson stops on second—a ground-rule double because the ball got caught under the snake slide, way over at the playground. Raymond is up next. While the fielder runs to get the ball, he takes two big cuts with the bat.

Jewel catches the ball, holds it ready, then throws. Raymond cracks it dead on and is around first base before Pinky, in the outfield, sees it coming her way.

Pinky does what I would do—she ducks—and the ball bounces over the back fence and onto the highway. A home run.

When Raymond stomps on home plate with both feet, Howie jumps up and down, rattling the chainlinks of the backstop. Raymond stands still and stares right at him. "What're you lookin' at?" he says. I take a few more steps to the side, moving out of Raymond's line of sight. He shakes his head. "Spaz."

"C'mon—who's up?" Jewel calls from the mound. It's my turn to bat, but Raymond hasn't moved from home plate.

"I'll be up," Howie offers, like he didn't hear what Raymond said.

Something bad is going to happen. I look over to the other side of the field, where a teacher stands by the tetherball pole, playground whistle dangling from her hand. She's too far away. I pick up the bat.

"I'll be up!" Howie says again.

Raymond turns his back on him. "You can't play," he says. "'Cause you're a moron."

By the way Howie's face dissolves, I know he heard this time. He pushes himself away from the backstop and lopes across the field. Joe runs after him. Howie is just a dot by the time he gets to the swings and slumps down on the grass.

I drop the bat in the dust. "Why do you *do* things like that?" I yell at Raymond before I can stop myself. "Howie never hurt anybody." I can feel my throat close up. *Oh, God. What am I doing?*

Raymond stares at me, his face closed. The other

kids are silent. I think of all the ways that Raymond could react, and I press my thumbs into my fists to keep from shaking. But I'm not sorry for what I said. Howie deserves to have somebody stick up for him.

⪻⪻⪻◎⫸⫸⫸

I'm in my bedroom changing out of my school clothes when Mom calls me back to the kitchen.

"Honey, I need you to go over to McKenzie's for some milk," she says. She pulls a dollar out of her wallet and sets it on the table.

It is only two blocks from our house, past the brick office building, then across the asphalt that spreads out from the store. People park wherever they want to, and I have to keep my eyes open so I don't get run over.

Mr. McKenzie sells groceries and a lot more — beads, buckskin and cradleboards, hardware and sporting goods. He has a museum of old photos, arrowheads, and baskets in the back. And the store is also the post office, so the back wall is covered with little glass-doored metal boxes, one for each family. One of the first things I learned at Warm Springs was how to twirl the knob to click open the combination lock — right 10, left 4, right 8 — to get our mail.

It is pretty quiet now, before the after-work rush. Just a few cars parked up next to the store, including a big station wagon with California plates. Two older men read their mail on the bench by the front door, leaning back in the sun that warms the concrete block wall. I push open the "In" door and then hold it for a mom wrestling a big bag of groceries in one arm and a toddler in the other. The lady says thanks, and the little boy gives me a one-tooth grin.

I'm thinking about how cute that kid is when I almost walk right into the rump of a big white woman in culottes. She looms over the single checkout counter, herding two scrawny kids. She holds two bottles of pop in one hand, money in the other, waiting to pay. I sidestep at the last second as a paunchy man comes up with a big bag of potato chips.

"Here, Marge — get this, too," he says, and pushes the bag into her arms. She juggles the stuff and scowls at him.

They're not from here. The California car must belong to them.

There's a crowd around the cash register, and then I see why. One red pomegranate sits on the counter, and a little girl who can barely see over the top is counting out pennies one by one. Jewel stands behind her, one hand on her shoulder.

Before Jewel sees me, I duck behind the magazine rack and go to the dairy case. When I come back up with the milk, nobody has moved.

The clerk, a high school kid, leans against the cash register, watching the little girl. He has rung up the purchase, but it doesn't look like she has enough money.

The lady with the pop gives an irritated sigh. "What's taking so long?" one of her kids whines.

"Can't you speed this up?" the lady asks the clerk. He just shrugs.

"Look," the man says, "we're in a hurry." Like that should make a difference.

The little girl pulls the last coin out of the handkerchief she has clutched in her hand. She puts it on the counter and looks up at the clerk.

"Not enough," he says. "You need five more cents."

"Good Lord!" says the man. He turns to his wife. "Marge, give the papoose a nickel so we can get out of here."

The little girl's eyes widen. I can just feel the quick thumping of her heart. Ignoring my own quickening pulse, I push past the fat man up to the counter. "Here." I shove the dollar at the clerk. "This will cover it."

He puts the milk and the change in a bag and hands it to me.

"*Hey, we were here first!*" the man bellows, but I whirl around and get myself right out the door.

I'm several quick paces across the parking lot when the door jingles open behind me. "Wait up!"

I turn. Jewel stands in the doorway, the little girl beside her. She hesitates, then they walk toward me. The little girl is clutching the fruit in her hand.

"Why'd you do that?" Jewel asks.

I don't know how to answer. A grownup should know better than to talk to a little kid like that. "Just wasn't right," I finally say.

The little girl reaches up and takes Jewel's hand, and her face seems to relax.

"Your sister?" I ask.

"My cousin," says Jewel. "Her name is Tela. She gets paid for chores at the boarding school. So we come get a treat on Fridays before we go home for the weekend." Tela gives me a shy smile.

The California family rushes out of the store without their bottles of pop. The kids are crying, and they pay no attention to us.

The sky is fading. At home, Mom is waiting for the milk. "I gotta go," I say.

"We owe you." Jewel points to the bag.

I shake my head. "Nah, it's my mom's money."

Jewel grins, nodding. The cousins cross the street and head back up to the school. As I start walking, I wonder who is coming to pick them up and how long it takes to get home. And I wonder what it's like to live away from your family so that you can go to school.

The station wagon peels out of the parking lot in a big hurry and screeches around the corner up toward the highway. *Good riddance,* Báshtan.

When I enter the kitchen, supper preparations are in full swing. Mom puts down the hamburger spatula and takes the sack. She looks inside, counts the change, and then looks at me.

"How much was the milk?" she asks.

I knew it. But I say only, "I bought a pomegranate."

Another quick glance back into the bag. "Where is it?"

For what feels like the first time in forever, I give her a big smile. "At the girls' dorm," I say, and go wash up.

The Old Ones

Mr. Nute plows down the aisle, handing out single-edge razor blades. Franklin follows him with squares of cardboard. On our desks, thin sheets of newspaper, *The Madras Pioneer,* are spread out under Dixie cups of tempera paint.

The social studies manual lies open on Mr. Nute's desk. Holding that fat book up in front of his face, he showed us the page with "Art of the Amazon" in big letters, after reading to us that Amazon tribesmen wore masks and little else. Mr. Nute says we understand a people through their art. He read that in there too.

Mr. Nute lays a blade on the newspaper that covers my desk.

"Be careful," he says out over my head. "Keep something under your work at all times. If you cut the desk, you'll be in big trouble."

Next to me, Pinky tilts her head. "What are we s'posed to do?"

I shrug. I don't want to draw Mr. Nute's attention. He has been stern with me ever since our conversation about Jewel.

I pick up the blade, careful to keep my fingers on the safe edge. I've never used a razor blade in art—or anywhere else, for that matter. This could be a *really* bad idea.

Mr. Nute picks up the teacher's manual and reads aloud, "Cut a diamond shape out of the cardboard. Make it big enough to cover your face."

The instant Mr. Nute starts talking, we start cutting. The cardboard is thick. The blades make a loud tearing sound as they work through it, drowning him out.

All of a sudden, Orin lets out a piercing shriek. All heads snap up. Mr. Nute drops the book and sprints over to Orin's desk.

Orin's head thrashes back and forth as Mr. Nute tries to capture his waving, spurting hand. *"Stop!"* Mr. Nute bellows. "You're getting *blood* on the *cardboard!*" Mr. Nute seizes Orin's bloody wrist and yanks him to his feet. The razor blade flies out of Orin's fingers and lands on Raymond's desk in the next row, spattering blood across the comics and Raymond's shirt.

"Geez!" yells Raymond, shoving himself backwards out of his seat. His foot catches on the desk leg, and he lands butt first in the aisle.

The gash in Orin's hand sprays blood across Mr. Nute's chest as he drags Orin across the room. They disappear out the door, and I hear Orin howling all the way down to Mr. Shanahan's office.

Raymond sits still for a second, then shakes himself off and gets back into his seat.

"Here. You can clean that up," says Pinky, handing him her handkerchief.

Raymond takes a couple of swipes at his shirt. Then he leans over, carefully picks up Orin's razor blade, and wipes it off on his knee.

During the rare times when we're left in the room alone, the class officers are supposed to take over. Benson calls out, "Hey! Where's the president?"

That's Orin.

"He's gone, you idiot," says Jewel. "So's Emerson." The vice president is spending the week in detention.

Everybody turns to Pinky. Only girls get elected secretary. You have to have nice handwriting.

"OK, then," she says, rising from her desk. "Let's

get out our library books and read until Mr. Nute comes back."

You'd think the kids would go wild, but everybody is glad to have routine to hang on to. Pinky gives a little smile and sits back down.

I fish for a book deep inside my desk. When I lower the lid, the cardboard diamond slides down, and I see what I've done. The newspaper is slashed clear across the livestock report.

I shove that aside and discover the half-dozen sharp, distinct stripes etched into the varnish. I have cut the desk.

I glance over at Pinky. She sees it too. "Oh, no! You heard what he said," she whispers.

Mr. Nute huffs himself back into the room alone, beads of sweat shining on his forehead. His shirtfront looks like he got caught in the sprinkler. He must have blotted out the blood in the teacher bathroom. Wet spots melt across his chest and round stomach.

"Put your heads down." This is how he handles a crisis.

I slap both palms over the cuts and plop my face down before anybody else has moved. I expect him to start yelling, but all I hear is one boot heel after the other pacing up and down in front of the room.

Pretty soon I hear steps coming down the hall. The boots stop marching over by the window and pivot to face the door. "Mr. Nute," Mr. Shanahan says, "we've sent him to the clinic. He'll need stitches." And then the quick steps recede back the way they came.

When he does speak, Mr. Nute's voice is tight. "Franklin, pick up the razor blades. *Nobody* else touch them. Benson, dump out the paint cups, and Kitty — you get the newspapers. The rest of you keep reading. Absolutely *no* talking." He sits down at his desk and picks up the *Pioneer* sports page that he had saved for himself.

I leave my book open on top of the scratches and go collect the newspapers. A wary quiet settles over the classroom.

There is not much left of the day. We put our library books in the bin, and Mr. Nute passes out spelling worksheets. He glowers through these final routines. His shirt is dry now, but you can still see faint splotches in the fabric.

When the last bell rings, Mr. Nute says, "Go home."

I know there is no way to hide my desk when I'm gone. I stuff the worksheet into my notebook and follow the crowd out of the room. I pluck my jacket from a coat hook in the hall and push through the big double doors.

Pinky catches up with me at the sidewalk. "Hey, why don't you come down to my house? We can do the spelling together."

I could use some company right now. "OK."

Mom won't care, as long as we're working on homework.

We take our usual route to the trail down to Pinky's house on Shitike Road. As we go, I think about that first time I worked my way down this hill, the day we went with Jimmy to the swimming hole and I met Raymond and Jewel. Everything was scary and strange back then. Now, each time I walk this way, I feel more at home. That eases some of the worry about Mr. Nute.

Pinky's house is small like ours. Neat, compact yard leading to a front porch. Big windows on either side of the door. A braided rug to wipe your feet. But it feels different—it has a "this is my house" feel. Not like the sameness of white paint and green shutters of the government houses on the upper campus, where I live.

Pinky throws the door open. "Mom," she calls out. "Kitty came home with me."

My eye is drawn to the large fireplace in the center of the front room. Something my house definitely doesn't have. Woven bags, tan and black, are spread out in a row on the mantel like in a museum. Figures on the bags resemble animals and birds. On the large bag at the end, a diamond shape looks like a face with large eyes. My cardboard mask would never have looked like this.

"My grandmother made them," Mrs. Wesley says behind me, pride in her voice. I turn and she is standing in the doorway, wiping her hands on a kitchen towel, her dark hair curling gently around her face. I'm almost as tall as she is, and I can see where Pinky gets the sparkle in her eyes. Her smile matches the voice I've come to know through the radio.

"Welcome," she says. Mrs. Wesley comes over to the fireplace, lifts the bag with the eyes, and hands it to me.

I turn it carefully. The face pattern is repeated all around the sides of the bag. "Who are these people?"

"The old ones," Mrs. Wesley says. "The ancestors who came before us." I think of Mrs. Queahpama sitting on our couch, telling me about the animals who were people.

"They're *beautiful*," I say, and her smile lifts the weight of the day off my shoulders.

A Whole Lot More Trouble

IN the morning, Pinky waits for me at the bottom of the school steps. I have my spelling done, all checked over. Mr. Nute will have no reason to look twice at me. But I didn't sleep very well.

"You look terrible," she says. "Still worried about the desk?"

"Well, yeah — wouldn't you be?"

"I'm telling you, he does not pay that much attention to us." Pinky steadies her books in the crook of one arm while sliding a bag of marbles into her pocket.

She isn't supposed to bring the marbles to school. She's already won every steelie and cat's-eye in the fifth and sixth grades. The boys put up such a fuss that Mr. Shanahan called her parents, and she was banned from the marbles ring at recess.

Pinky wore the ban as a badge of honor for a few weeks, until the boys got cocky and begged her to play so they could win back what they'd lost. She's cleaned out about half of them again. This time, they're too embarrassed to tell on her.

The scratches did not magically disappear overnight. I see them as soon as I walk into the classroom. I set my tablet on top of them and pick up the bin of library books we collected yesterday afternoon. I'm class librarian this week, a helpful distraction right now. I drag the bin down the hall.

The main office door is open, and so is the inner door to Mr. Shanahan's office. He's pacing in front of the doorway, and I hear his voice, loud and angry. Mr. Nute sits in the same chair where I sat in October. He's looking down at the floor, like a kid when the teacher is ranting.

I ease my way past, careful not to catch Mr. Shanahan's eye. Then I hear him say, "Why on earth would you give them *razor blades?*"

I hustle the book bin into the library and get back to class as the first bell rings. Pinky picks up the roll sheet, calls out, "OK, say 'here' if you're here," and reads off the names.

But Mr. Nute still does not show up. Pinky pokes Dora, the flag salute leader, and we all recite the pledge.

Finally, Mr. Nute thumps through the doorway. He looks downright surly. He doesn't thank Pinky or apologize for being late. He just says, "Get out your math books."

Mr. Nute pulls his teacher's manual out from under the mess on his desk and quickly scrawls a string of page numbers on the board. The continued torture of dividing fractions.

"Do the odd problems on these pages," he says. Then he stands at the window, his back to the room.

As the clock ticks toward the end of the day, I wonder how much longer I can hide the scratches from him. At three o'clock we clear our desks and go home.

Pinky and I have walked a couple of blocks when I tell her I'm going back. I have to get it over with.

"You want me to come with you?"

"Yeah—but I have to do this on my own."

When I go back into the classroom, Mr. Nute is sitting at his desk staring at a piece of paper in his hand. He looks up, his eyes dark.

He knows. I stand there like a dope.

I breathe in, then say, "I'm very sorry, Mr. Nute."

"It's over," he says, his voice flat.

He mustn't tell my parents. Never in a million years

would they expect something like this from me. My throat starts to close up.

"I didn't mean to," I whisper.

Mr. Nute frowns. *"What?"*

"My desk. I . . . I didn't mean to cut it."

Mr. Nute just stares at me. And then something comes across his face, and he begins to laugh, a cackle that starts in the back of his throat and rises over the room. He sounds like a crazy person. I back up until my hands find the side of the door.

When he calms down, Mr. Nute pulls out his handkerchief and wipes his eyes. "You think *that* matters?" he asks, shaking his head.

"Mr. Nute," I say finally, "is something wrong?"

He sits there. Then he holds up that piece of paper. "I'm done," he says. "Fired."

Mr. Nute is in a whole lot more trouble than I am.

Consider Your Sins

SURE enough, the classroom is empty on Monday morning. Except for Jewel and Dora going through Mr. Nute's desk.

"What are you *doing?*" I ask.

"Told you he's gone," Dora says to Jewel.

I set my stuff on my desk, check the doorway, and go up to the front of the room.

"Look," says Jewel, and she pulls open the top drawer. Not even a pencil shaving or a paper clip. Same for the big file drawers at the side, and the bookcase behind the desk has been cleared out too. "Where'd he go?" she asks.

"Don't know and don't care," says Dora with a grin. "We got rid of him."

I am off the hook, but the way it happened doesn't bring the relief I was hoping for.

"I wonder who we'll get this time," Jewel says.

Any new teacher should be an improvement.

"What are you girls doing in here?" A voice snatches me back to Earth, and I slowly turn to face it.

A woman fills the doorway. Not fat so much as tall and bosomy. Brown plaid dress with a teacher sweater draped over straight shoulders. Trim hair and old-lady shoes, even though she looks about my mom's age. She has a clipboard tucked under one arm, a stack of books cradled in the other.

"Excuse me. Do you not hear well?" She tilts her head to glare at us over her glasses.

"I'm sorry!" pops right out of my mouth. "We...uh ...were trying to find Mr. Nute."

"In his desk?"

"No."

"No?" she repeats.

"No, I mean..." I glance sideways at Jewel. *Help me out here!* She stares off like she is no longer in the room. "We don't have any business up here," I say quietly.

The woman nods, as if to say *Good answer,* and hangs the clipboard on the hook by the door. "Go on outside until the bell rings."

Fifteen minutes later, the class files into the room.

The new teacher's sweater hangs on the peg, and thick books fill up the shelves. Her name is written on the blackboard in elegant script — *Miss Anthony*. And below it, displayed in the center of the chalk tray, a black leather book with gold lettering. A Bible.

We settle into our seats and wait. Before she takes roll — or wishes us good morning, even — Miss Anthony stands at the front of the room and hugs that Bible to her chest. "Bow your heads, children," she says.

"Heavenly Father," she whispers, "bless our minds and our hearts so that we may glorify Your work here on Earth. Amen."

"Amen," I respond automatically.

Then I remember that teachers are not supposed to pray. The Supreme Court said so last summer. Miss Anthony doesn't seem to care that the first thing we do in her class is illegal.

I wonder what else we're in for.

⋘◄◙►⋙

At recess, Benson reports that the Nutes' house is all cleared out. On Sunday night he saw the moving van pull away from the street where the teachers live, just west of school, and turn left at the highway.

"Back to the city, where he belongs," Benson crows on his way to the backstop.

Pinky shakes her head. "That was quick. And where'd *she* come from?" Nobody seems to know.

When the lunch bell finally rings, I grab my jacket off the hook and hurry home. They're already talking about it when I come in the back door. At least, I think that's what "reassigned to Alaska" means.

Dad looks up from his sandwich. "Meet your new teacher?" he asks.

"Yeah — Miss Anthony." He doesn't need to know how.

"Me too," says Joe. "We were in the hall this morning, and this *huge* lady stared so hard at Miss Tutwiler, she turned around and shushed us. We were just *walking!*"

"You're not supposed to make noise in the halls," I point out.

"Yeah, but nobody ever *says* so."

"Who is she?" I ask Dad.

"Miss Anthony arrived last week to help out up at the Baptist mission."

I can picture it: *New mission lady drives the church van, capturing little kids for Bible class.* I'll spare him the part about the Bible this morning. He'd have a fit that a teacher prayed in school.

Dad pushes back from the table and sets his plate on the counter. "Then a spot suddenly opened up at the school. Miss Anthony is a teacher, Pastor Leland said something about the greater good, and...well..." He heads down the steps to the back door. "You already know the rest."

When I arrive at the playfield after lunch, there's a big knot of kids at the backstop. Baseball happens every day, even when the wind is biting, like today. But nobody's playing now. The kids are all standing with their heads down, and Miss Anthony is towering over them. The scene has Howie Granger written all over it.

"Where's the retarded boy?" she asks as I come up to the back of the crowd.

Nobody says anything. Her gaze sweeps onto Orin, who is closest. "I'm told he likes to play baseball. Is he part of the game?"

Orin glances at Raymond. Miss Anthony's eyes shift to him too. "Hmm?"

"No," Raymond says, looking past the fence.

"Why not?"

"Doesn't want to."

"I see," Miss Anthony says. "Any idea why that might be so?"

When Raymond doesn't respond, she snaps her fingers. "Lunch is over. Get back to your classrooms."

Miss Anthony turns and blasts the whistle as she

waves the other kids in, her arm pointed toward the school. I glance around for Howie, but he is long gone. And it looks like Raymond got caught this time.

Back in the classroom, Miss Anthony doesn't seem to be in a hurry. She hangs the whistle on the hook by the door. She pushes the sleeves of her sweater up her forearms. She settles her glasses squarely on her nose and then stands in front of us, arms folded, and begins. "Who can tell me what happened out there?"

Instinct tells me it is better not to volunteer. I keep my eyes focused on the worn groove holding a pencil at the top of my scarred desk.

Miss Anthony walks slowly through the back rows. After three or four passes, she finally speaks from the back of the room. "Howie is one of the Lord's special creatures." *There she goes again, talking about God.*

"We'll take a moment of silence now. Every one of you needs to search your heart and consider why you are so mean."

In the quiet, I think about Howie. He flaps his hands when he talks, and I can't always understand him. I know he can't help it, but he almost invites kids to pick on him. This is probably not what Miss Anthony expects me to be thinking about.

She strides to the front of the room to grab her Bible from the chalk tray. She stands in front of us and talks directly to Raymond. "When you are cruel, you only hurt yourself," she says. "And you *will* learn to spread compassion to others."

I wonder how she pegged Raymond as the tormentor so quickly.

"Please come up here." This is a command, not a request.

Surprised, Raymond stands up and slowly walks to the front of the room.

"Turn around and face the class," she says.

He obeys. Slowly.

Miss Anthony closes her eyes and moves her lips for a few seconds. Then she deftly flicks the hand that holds her Bible, and the book falls open.

"We'll begin with Proverbs eleven five," she says, flipping pages with her finger. She holds the Bible out to Raymond. "This is about you. Read it."

He hesitates, and I wonder if he dares to refuse.

Then he takes the book, bends his head toward the page, and reads. "'The righteousness of the blameless keeps his way straight, but the wicked falls by his own wickedness.'"

There is no other sound in the room, no movement. I can't imagine how it feels for Raymond to stand up there in front of all of us. I don't know if I could take it like he does.

I glance at Jewel a couple of rows over. She sits with her head down, eyes closed, fists clenched on her knees.

Miss Anthony takes the Bible out of Raymond's hands. She flips a few more pages. "And in chapter seventeen we learn that 'he who is glad at calamity will not go unpunished.'" She presses her palms together and the book snaps shut.

"Sit down," Miss Anthony says to Raymond, "and consider your sins."

I can't believe she would humiliate him this way. Raymond walks slowly down the aisle, his head up and eyes fixed straight ahead. He looks completely unmoved.

Miss Anthony talks about compassion, but she sure doesn't show any. I almost feel sorry for him.

A Rose Deep Red in a Circle of White

AT the top of an endless hour before lunch, Miss Anthony picks up a long piece of chalk. She flips it between two fingers to hold like a cigarette as she adjusts her glasses. Turning her back to us, she begins to plant division problems on the board.

"Copy these and do them," she says as she writes.

A few minutes later, a shadow grows in the doorway beside my desk. It's Mr. Reeser, the janitor. "'Scuse me, Miss Anthony," he says.

Her hand freezes on a 5. She turns only her head toward him. "Ronald."

"Mr. Shanahan asked me to move some furniture in the attic. I'm taking a couple of boys to help. Might get a little noisy overhead."

She's not going to like that. Miss Anthony doesn't believe in noise. Sure enough, she ignores him and turns back to the board to finish the last problem.

I didn't know this school had an attic. I wish I could see it. I imagine a stale, dusty room full of old desks with broken seats. File cabinets of lost records, or maybe books with swear words scribbled in the margins.

Miss Anthony scans the classroom. She plucks victims one by one to wrestle the problems at the board. We're supposed to keep one eye on them while working out the problems at our desks. You have to be ready to go up and do it right when somebody stumbles. She says it's good practice. It also causes bad feelings.

Miss Anthony patrols the board, peering over the sweaty heads as the kids work with their backs to the room. Then she looks out at the rest of us and settles on me. "Kitty. It's your turn. Fix Raymond's for him."

I definitely do not want to do that. "Miss Anthony," I say, "I'm not done yet."

All the way back to his seat, Raymond's eyes are fixed on me. If I do what she says, I'll pay for it at recess.

"You're done enough. Get up there," Miss Anthony says as she marches down the line from Raymond's empty spot at the board. She holds out her hand to Orin, and he gives up his chalk like a losing pitcher yanked from the mound.

I try again. "I'll do Orin's."

"Raymond's," she says.

I can see what a mess he has made on the board, the problem smeared by a wet palm.

I sigh and get out of my seat. Arguing with Miss Anthony never works. It's always her way or no way.

I have to walk right by Raymond's desk. He stares down at his worksheet, pencil in hand, but I can't miss what he says under his breath. "Go ahead. See what happens."

I take a quick step and grab the chalk out of the tray. I stall some more by rewriting the numbers as evenly and carefully and small as I can. Then I stand there, not sure how to do the problem.

Miss Anthony's voice sinks down onto the back of my neck. "You *were* listening when we learned this, weren't you?"

Such a dangerous question with no safe answer.

Suddenly, I hear an invasion of giant, hard-soled rats rattling and bumping above my head. Something heavy is being dragged across the ceiling.

Miss Anthony's head snaps up. *"Good Lord!"* She reaches out to steady herself on my shoulder and lets go an instant later when the ceiling explodes with a sharp crack. Plaster splatters all over my desk as everybody ducks for cover.

I look up to see a kid's pant leg and sneakered foot dangling from a jagged hole in the ceiling. Somebody must have pulled him to safety, as the shoe disappears.

In seconds, Mr. Reeser appears in the doorway, his face white. Then Mr. Shanahan pushes through. "What *happened?*" he asks Miss Anthony.

She shrugs. "Children do not belong in the attic," she says calmly. "It's dangerous." Like he should have known better.

Mr. Shanahan considers the mess. "We need to clean this up," he says to Mr. Reeser.

"Yes, you do," says Miss Anthony, as the noon bell rings. "We will go to lunch now and be back promptly at one o'clock."

With half the ceiling sprayed across the room, I don't see how they'll get it cleaned up in an hour. But that's not my problem. *My* problem is staying out of Raymond's way. Just my luck that today Mom decides to go visit a friend in Madras and I have to eat lunch at school.

Miss Anthony marches our straggly line out the front door. I duck in behind her and stick close all the way across the playfield to the dining hall. I want to stay as far away from Raymond as possible. I have no idea what he might do, but I'm not taking any chances.

Shorty, the cook, looks up when his big doors swing open.

"Mr. Walsey." Miss Anthony gives a curt nod. "We've had a *situation,* and we are here early for lunch."

Shorty grins. "Well, today you're in luck. We got plenty of meatballs!"

"Thank you." Miss Anthony motions for me to hold the door open.

Oh, man! Now I have to stand here while everybody passes by. Including Raymond. I'm thinking maybe I can yank Pinky out of line to protect me, but just then Miss Anthony holds out her hand like a cop and stops the line from moving forward.

"Raymond," she calls, "come hand out the milk cartons." This is Raymond's regular job. He has to wear a hairnet and everything.

Raymond is slouching against the concrete wall of the dining hall, hands in his pockets. He pushes himself away from the wall, elbows Orin to the side, and comes up the steps.

❯❯❯❮❮❮

It is unusually quiet in the dining hall when I pull the doors shut and pick up a tray. The few times I've eaten here, I've been surprised by the racket that a roomful of kids with metal trays can make. Now all I hear is

Shorty at the far end of the line cheerfully spooning up spaghetti and sauce. The kids don't jostle and clank like they normally do as they wait for food. As I reach for a fork and spoon, some of the boys are already banging out through the doors to the playground. Miss Anthony is nowhere in sight.

In his spot handing out the milk, Raymond sets one carton on each tray that passes. Nobody has the nerve to tease him, even with a net thing mashing down his hair.

Jewel is the last person ahead of me in line. Her ponytail hangs far down her back, held in place with a beaded clip. A rose deep red in a circle of white. This is the first time I've been close enough to see the delicate lines of pink that form folds in the petals, the tiny gold beads framing the outline. The work is tight and perfectly even. *Someone must really care for her to make something so beautiful.*

Raymond pushes milk across the counter and onto her tray. "Leave her alone," Jewel says to him. "She didn't do anything to you." Then she slides her tray on down the line.

I follow fast behind her. Jewel sets her tray down at an empty table. She climbs over the bench, sits, and begins to pick through the food.

I hesitate, standing behind her with my tray. "Were you talking about me?"

Jewel glances over at Raymond. He has whipped off that hair net and is hunching over his tray at the far end of the next table.

"Yes," she says.

Thoughts are swirling in my head. Raymond makes fun of Howie and threatens me. But Miss Anthony picks on him. Now Jewel is sticking up for me. I don't know who is on which side, but I'm grateful for her help.

"Thank you," I tell her.

The Dressing

We're eating breakfast in the kitchen when a long black car passes the window. Then an open truck full of people follows close behind. Women sit on benches in the back against the wooden slats, dark scarves tied over their heads, arms holding their shawls close in the cold December morning. Their wailing reaches the place where I sit with a piece of toast in my hand.

Mom stops short of the table, holding a pan of oatmeal. We watch the long line of cars and pickups now passing slowly by our house.

"What happened?" I ask.

Standing over by the sink, Dad drinks the last of his coffee. He has his boots on, so he must be headed out to the woods today. "Car accident, honey."

"Was somebody hurt?" I see Mom's eyes meet his.

"That was a hearse," Bill says. "A girl fell out the back of a pickup."

"Oh," I say, putting down my spoon. *She's dead.* I can't eat any more.

Mom puts her hand on my shoulder. "The people in the truck are mourners—they're going with her down to the longhouse. Remember—where we were invited to the service?"

I do. The drumming and singing were so different from what happens in our church, but powerful, too. I hope it helps this little girl. I leave the table to get ready for school.

On the way out the door, Bill lets me catch up with him. "How did you know about the girl?" I ask. I hold my books in one arm, zip up my jacket, and pull the sleeves down over my hands. The December morning is clear and biting. The sunrise glows against the rim-rock at the top of the canyon but has not yet touched the bottom.

Bill swings the glove he carries to junior high every day, baseball season or not. "I heard them talking. It came over the radio yesterday. Dad was telling Mom about it."

"Do you know where?"

"I think it was the Simnasho road. The truck skidded on a patch of ice."

"Who was it?"

He shrugs. "Some little kid." He sprints off to catch the bus.

I turn toward the school, crossing the street and stepping over the cable strung between low posts surrounding the campus. The only time I've been in the back of a truck was last summer when Mrs. Queahpama picked us up on Shitike Road. I know it's dangerous to ride in a pickup bed, and I'm glad that my parents want to keep us safe. But it was so much fun. Out there in the dry wind and spicy smell of the sagebrush, I could see everything. Feel each grate on the cattle guard, all the rattles of that gravel road. I can imagine cows and dogs and magpies speaking to me. The cold or heat wrapping me up.

Other kids do it all the time. When I go to McKenzie's store for the mail or some milk, kids are climbing in or out of the backs of trucks. They pass us by in a spray of dust as we pedal our bikes on Shitike Road. Families park their pickups across from our house when they go to the tribal offices next door. Sometimes the grandmas climb down and spread blankets on our grass and wait there with the little kids.

But this little girl fell out of the back, and she died. I'm walking slowly up the sidewalk toward the school, and awful pictures push their way into my head. In slow motion, a child slides toward the side of the truck bed as wheels slip on the ice. She can't hang on. She is flung into the air as the truck skids and slams into the ditch, her dad pounding the brake, her sisters clawing for something to hold on to.

She must have been terrified. In my head, her sisters are screaming. And then suddenly I'm back in Warm Springs on a Thursday morning, late for school.

The halls are quiet when I open the front door and hurry down to the classroom. I ease into my desk as Miss Anthony is taking roll.

Jewel is not in her seat on the far side of the room. Several desks are empty, including Raymond's. I wonder if they know this little girl.

Maybe they were in the cars that followed the hearse and the truck full of mourners this morning, turning at McKenzie's where the road curves down the hill, across Shitike Creek, toward the longhouse.

Miss Anthony clips the attendance sheet to the doorway for one of the office helpers to collect. She picks up her Bible from the chalk tray like she does every morning. "Some of you know that we have had a death in this school," she says. "Today I'm going to read my favorite psalm. Please bow your heads and listen."

I can feel the Valley of the Shadow of Death, and it feels like the steep draws full of juniper and sagebrush on the way to Simnasho. A curvy road that ices up in the winter, and you can't see the danger until you hit it. Where little girls fly up out of pickup beds and don't come back.

◄◄◄►HOH►►►

All morning, we work on poems for the Christmas pageant. Tomorrow night, the parents will crowd into a gym transformed by sparkly lights and tinsel. We'll recite our poems and then go home for the break that is always the next best thing to summer vacation.

I can only pretend to write. My head is full of questions, not Christmas. Did her family have to see her lying in the road? Did she know what was coming? Was she cold?

I imagine yesterday when the radio squawked to life in the hall, the police signing in and telling the story in code.

"We got a ten forty-two on the Simnasho road." *Traffic accident.*

"What's your ten-twenty?" *Where are you?*

"Milepost eight. At the curve by the river."

"Ten thirty-eight?" *Need an ambulance?*

There would be a pause. Then "No...ten-five the coroner." *Relay message.*

"Ten-four. Over and out."

I walk home by myself at noon. The trees stretch their bare branches around the campus as if they're begging for spring. From the street, I can see my family through the kitchen window.

"Mary Ann dropped by this morning," Mom is saying to Dad as I come in. "She was on her way to the longhouse for the dressing." Mary Ann is Mrs. Sahme, one of Mom's friends.

"The funeral's tomorrow?" he asks.

Mom nods. "She told me I would be welcome. But I don't think I could go. A child..." She shakes her head and sits down.

Dressing? I want to ask her about it, but my dad starts talking about work and I stop listening.

A moment later, I realize that they're both waiting for me. "Her cousins?" Mom asks again. "I think they're in your class. Those kids who live at Simnasho but stay at the boarding school."

All those empty desks this morning. Jewel and Raymond. And then I see the small hand reaching over the counter at McKenzie's to offer a last penny that will not be enough. *Tela.* My stomach squeezes tight.

Mom puts her hand over mine on the table. "Did you know her?" she asks gently.

I can only nod, blinking hard to hold the tears in place.

As we walk back to school, Joe chatters about the song his class is rehearsing for the pageant. I know that he is trying to cheer me up, but I can't listen. I'm watching the clouds where a little girl lies still, her arms folded across her chest. God and Jesus and the angels comb her hair. They smooth down the skirt of her dress and pull her knee socks straight. This makes me feel a whole lot better than the Twenty-third Psalm did.

≪≪≪HO╫≫≫≫

After supper, Mom cleans up the kitchen while we kids help Dad finish decorating the Christmas tree he brought from the woods. When we're done, Bill and Joe go brush their teeth. I stay put. I sit close to Dad on the sofa, rest my cheek against the soft sleeve of his shirt. He smells like pipe tobacco and the woods.

I watch him lean over the coffee table to pick up his pipe. He taps the cold ashes into the ashtray and opens the yellow pouch he keeps in his back pocket. He carefully packs new tobacco into the bowl—a steady and calm ritual that has always been a part of my life.

"Dad?"

"Mmm-hmm," he answers, his teeth steadying the pipe for the lighted match.

"What's a dressing?"

He pulls air slowly in as the tobacco catches, then lets the smoke go. The sweet richness settles over me. In the seconds when he doesn't say anything, I imagine him checking through all the conversations he has had today, searching for one that fits my question.

"You mean the funeral?"

"Yes. What Mrs. Sahme said about Tela."

"Oh." He leans back on the sofa and puts his big arm around me. I pull up my feet and tuck myself close to him. "When somebody dies, people go to the long-house to help get her ready to be buried. Someone close to her will bring new clothes and dress her in them."

Like God and Jesus on the cloud.

He hugs me. "People sit with the family and help them, too."

"Did you do that with Grandpa?"

"No, not quite that way. We took clothes to the funeral home and the undertaker dressed Grandpa."

He puffs quietly, and finally I ask him, "Does it hurt?"

Dad looks at me. His other hand comes over and gently pushes my bangs out of my eyes.

"She didn't feel it, honey," he says quietly. "It was very fast. She didn't even know what was happening."

I can barely make the next words come out. "Was she all by herself?"

I'm afraid to know, but I have to ask. And my dad says what I need to hear. "Somebody was with her the whole time."

A Good Thing

WHEN the Christmas vacation is over, most of the kids come back and fill up the desks. Not Raymond and Jewel. I keep watch over their empty seats as the days add up. The school feels heavy in the new year. Quiet settles over the halls and the playground, and we wait.

Miss Anthony carries on with our usual routines, acting as if she doesn't feel the thread of tension pulled tight around the classroom. At the beginning of the second week, she comes up to me as I turn around in my seat for the millionth time to see if Jewel is back yet.

"You have to keep your mind on your work," she says, resting her hand on my shoulder for one brief second.

This morning, Pinky waits for me at the bottom of the school steps.

"It's time to get things back to normal," she says.

I can see her point. The heavy sadness is hard to live with day after day.

When we walk into the classroom before school, there's Jewel. She stands to the side of Miss Anthony's desk, waiting for our teacher to talk to her. Right away, I see what's different about her. This is not the same fierce girl who kept us from the swimming hole last summer, or who stood up to Mr. Nute.

Jewel stands there with her head down, as if it is too heavy for her neck to hold. Her clothes are rumpled, her blouse pulled out of her skirt. And her hair is held back in a tangled ponytail wrapped with just a rubber band. The beautiful beaded clip is gone. *She's mourning, and nobody is taking care of her.*

I back away from the doorway. "We need to let her talk to Miss Anthony," I say quietly. Pinky follows me back outside.

When the morning bell finally rings and everyone jostles into the classroom, Jewel sits alone at her desk. Kids move carefully, quietly, around her. Miss Anthony stands at the blackboard, putting the finishing touches on the daily schedule.

The entire day goes by as if we are mired in quick-sand. When the final bell rings, it feels as if I let go the breath I've been holding all day. Kids push out through the doorway.

I keep watching Jewel, who has hardly moved. Her head still down, she tiredly pushes herself away from her desk and stands up slowly. She doesn't take anything with her, just turns for the door.

"Your parents must meet with me," Miss Anthony says. "To explain your absence."

Jewel raises her head. She looks confused.

"Even with the Christmas vacation," Miss Anthony says. "You missed too many days."

I stop near the doorway, fiddling with the zipper on my jacket. Everybody else has gone. Jewel glances at me, then back down at the floor.

I know I have no business getting involved, but Miss Anthony doesn't understand. "There was the funeral," I say. I'm scared but I keep going. "The family needs time to take care of everything."

Miss Anthony's eyes narrow. "Kitty," she says, "you need to get on home now."

Jewel's look says, *Leave me alone.*

"I'm sorry, Miss Anthony," I say. "I thought you would want to know." And then I go.

Jewel drifts through the days. She stares at her desk most of the time, not even trying to follow what we're doing in class. At lunch and out on the playground, she stays by herself and doesn't talk to anybody. She looks lost and alone. I want to help her, but I don't know how.

Miss Anthony watches too. She keeps glancing over at Jewel's desk like she is about to say something. She never calls Jewel's name or speaks to her, though it might help if she did.

Raymond stays away, and nobody talks about him. Pinky says people often miss a lot of work or school when somebody dies. I wonder if that's what makes Miss Anthony so stern.

When the clock ticks to three and the last bell rings, Jewel is the first one out the door. I have to scratch around inside my desk to find my math book.

Pinky waits for me in the hall, her coat on and buttoned. "Wanna do the homework at my house?" she asks.

I shake my head. "Mom told me to come straight home. She's got chores for me."

When we push through the double doors, I spot Jewel sitting on one of the swings at the far end of the playfield. No coat, no books, just pushing herself slowly back and forth with her toes.

I'm about to use Mom as an excuse to myself for not going over. I won't know what to say. But I can't leave Jewel to go on all by herself.

"Let's go talk to her." I start across the street. "C'mon."

Jewel looks up when we get close. She wipes her nose with the back of her hand, then takes her sleeve and wipes her eyes.

I walk over and sit down in the swing next to her. Pinky stands off to the side, her hand on the cold steel pole. I have no idea what to do now, so I just swing gently.

Then Pinky says quietly over the top of Jewel's head, "I'm so sorry about your cousin."

She said just the right thing. And it's so simple.

Jewel sniffs, then tilts her head down, shutting us out. But she doesn't move or get up to leave. I keep rocking back and forth.

Finally, Jewel looks up. "I miss her," she says simply. And then she sighs from somewhere deep inside. Her voice is so tired and lonely that the sadness surges in my chest, then spreads up through my neck to pulse behind my eyes.

Pinky asks, "And Raymond?"

"He's still with *Káthla*." Jewel shrugs. "Won't come back to school. Won't get out of bed. Won't talk."

It's hard to imagine Raymond caring so much about anyone. He must be hurting too.

"Like last time?" Pinky asks.

Jewel nods her head slowly. "Yeah. Just like ..." Her voice trails off, and she stops.

What does she mean? And who is Cutla? But I keep the questions to myself.

"Miss Anthony says *Káthla* has to come to school tomorrow," Jewel says.

The playfield is empty. All the kids have gone home or into the dormitories. The sun slants down on us, sliding into the west. The light is weak and soft, and I'm glad I have my jacket. Jewel must be cold out here with nothing around her shoulders.

"I gotta go," Jewel says finally. She stands up from the swing and I do too. Jewel turns toward the girls' dorm, behind us.

"Wait." Jewel stops and looks back at me. It seems so little, but I have to say it. "I'm sorry too."

"She liked you," Jewel says. "Back there at the store that time?"

I see that little hand reach up and place the last coin

on the counter. And outside, in the parking lot, fold itself into Jewel's.

"You did a good thing," she says.

Tears fill my eyes, and I can only nod my thanks. Jewel heads across the playfield and up the broad front steps of the dorm, then slips through the doors.

Káthla

ALL through the next day, I watch the doorway for someone to come talk to Miss Anthony about Jewel. Maybe I'll see her parents. But aside from the girl who picks up the attendance and Mr. Shanahan popping in for a quick and muffled conversation with Miss Anthony, nobody enters the classroom. Jewel stays focused on her desk, her face etched with sorrow.

At the end of the day, Miss Anthony slaps a math test onto my desk, her index finger pinned to the big, red D at the top.

"*You* can do better," she says. "Go clean this up before you leave."

"Clean this up" means I have to stay after class and do the missed problems over. Show all my work and make it neat. No erasing, no cross-outs. I snatch up the test and my pencil and settle in at the work table in the back of the room.

Movement in the hall catches my eye. A tiny, ancient woman stands at the doorway, holding her wool jacket close over a dark wing dress, a black scarf tied back over braided gray hair. It's Mrs. Queahpama. *What is she doing here?*

Behind her, Raymond slumps in the shadows.

Miss Anthony finally notices her, and Mrs. Queahpama takes a step inside. "I've come to talk about my grandchildren," she says.

Káthla?

For a second, Miss Anthony looks surprised. Then she quickly gathers herself. "We are not yet finished for the day," she says. "You can wait for me in the school office, if you like."

"I will wait here." Mrs. Queahpama takes off her jacket and settles herself on a chair beside the door. Raymond stays out in the hall, leaning between the coat hooks, his arms crossed and his head down.

Miss Anthony turns away from her and passes out the rest of the tests. The bell rings as I yank a clean sheet of paper out of the stack Miss Anthony keeps on the work table for do-overs.

Out of the corner of my eye, I watch Jewel stop at the doorway and stand beside her grandmother. When all the other kids are gone, Mrs. Queahpama motions Raymond into the room, and he trades one wall for another.

Miss Anthony takes her time putting books away, erasing the board. Then she turns around and leans against her desk. "Now," she says, "thank you for coming to meet with me."

Mrs. Queahpama nods. Miss Anthony picks up her grade book and studies it for a minute, counting.

"Jewel missed eight days before the Christmas vacation," she says. "Raymond has missed twice as many. Frankly, they're not bright enough to miss so much school."

Did she just call them stupid? I melt down low in my seat, hoping Jewel won't see me. I don't want her to be shamed in front of me.

"We have had a great loss," Mrs. Queahpama says quietly. "The children need time."

"These children need to be in school." Miss Anthony frowns. "It's their parents' responsibility to see that they return to the dormitories so that they do not fall so far behind."

Mrs. Queahpama rises slowly from her chair. Standing, she is shorter than Raymond and Jewel, but she seems to fill the room. Though her voice remains soft, there is iron inside it. "There are things more important than school."

Miss Anthony shakes her head and crosses her arms. "It is our policy," she says firmly, "that boarding students attend regularly if they expect the privilege of residing here. Raymond is in serious jeopardy of being dismissed from the dormitory."

Mrs. Queahpama looks at her grandchildren, then back at Miss Anthony. "Yes, I know how this school works." She nods. "That is why I signed them out of the dorms. They will be coming to stay with me."

Jewel jerks her head to catch her grandmother's eye. Her face looks softer, relieved. I don't know what changed, but I'm happy to see it.

Miss Anthony does not let go. "I'm sure that is a decision for their parents to make."

Jewel and Raymond turn anxious eyes to their grandmother, and I wonder why. Mrs. Queahpama looks at our teacher for a moment without speaking. Then she picks up her wool jacket and works her arm into it. Jewel holds the sleeve for her, pats the shoulder smooth. "Let's go home," Mrs. Queahpama says.

After they leave, Miss Anthony finally sees me. "Finish that at home," she says. I quickly gather my things and get out of there.

At the end of the hall, Raymond and Jewel are standing outside the office door. I see that Mrs. Queahpama is inside, talking with Mr. Shanahan at the counter.

I stand so that Jewel is between me and Raymond. "You don't have to live at school anymore?" I ask her.

Jewel nods. "My *káthla* is taking us to stay with her. She lives past McKenzie's store, out near the highway."

I want to ask about her parents, but that feels wrong somehow.

Jewel picks at her fingernails, not looking at me. "You heard what she said about us back there?" She tilts her head toward the classroom down the hall.

"I didn't hear anything," I say. It's not the truth, but I don't care.

Jewel smiles a tiny bit, like she knows what I'm doing.

"See you Monday," I tell her, and walk on home.

The Worst of It

AND just like that, something lifts. March arrives, and spring begins to tease us as the days warm with smells of sagebrush climbing up the mesa across the highway, the feathery cottonwoods budding out down by Shitike Creek, the musk of the first mown grass on the campus. Miss Anthony keeps the windows open most afternoons, even with the highway so close.

With every week that passes, Jewel seems more at ease. Raymond remains mostly silent, but he's no longer so hostile. He just looks empty. They don't always get to school on time, but they get there. And they walk home to their *káthla*'s every afternoon, crossing the campus and cutting the corner by our house to take the short-cut up the alley.

I watch for them from our kitchen, where I sit after

school telling Mom about the day. Raymond always strides in front, head down and hands in his pockets as Jewel follows him with books. I'm glad they have each other.

On Wednesday, Mom is stepping out the back door when I come around the house after school. "Oh, good, you're home," she says, holding out a stack of letters with stamps. "Would you take these to the mail for me?"

I've got a ton of homework. "Can't you send one of the boys?" I ask.

"Bill's not home yet, and Joe's got Cub Scouts in ten minutes. I need these to go out today."

I sigh to let her know what a burden this is. Then I set my stuff on the back steps and take the letters.

There is the usual jumble of cars and trucks parked outside McKenzie's, shopping carts abandoned in the parking lot. I wind my way through them and push open the glass doors. It smells like smoked meat and old wood in here from the worn floor and the jars of beef jerky at the checkout counter. I love that smell.

I ease my way among the people and carts crowding the aisles, walk toward the metal bank of postboxes lining one wall at the back of the building. When I come around a counter loaded with strings of beads, I see Jewel stretching up on her tiptoes, reaching to a high box. She pulls out an envelope.

"Hey," I say.

Jewel looks up. "*Káthla* says this is the best part about us staying with her. She can't reach the mailbox."

This is the most normal kid thing she has ever said to me. As if we're friends. *Maybe we are?*

"How is it—being out of the dorm?" I ask.

Jewel thinks about this for a moment, then she smiles. "It's like we're finally home." She looks so relaxed.

She turns to close the little door on the postbox, and I see the deep red rose made of beads in her hair. Now I'm sure that things are better for her.

"You're wearing your hair clip again," I say, though I'm kind of scared that she'll think this is none of my business.

Jewel puts her hand to the back of her ponytail and touches the beads. "*Káthla* made this for me a few years ago," she says, her voice suddenly quiet. "At a sad time. She wanted me to know that she loved me."

"It's beautiful."

I drop Mom's letters through the slot, and we walk outside together. A breeze rustles the poplars around the campus, spinning dust across the parking lot. The late-afternoon air is warm.

"Maybe you could come over some day after school," I say quickly, hoping she doesn't laugh.

Jewel considers this for a second. Then she says, "Yeah, OK." Just like friends making plans.

"How come you don't hang out with Norma anymore?" I hadn't meant to ask this, but it's been on my mind.

Jewel looks thoughtful and kind of sad. "When we lost my cousin, I started to see how mean Norma is. People like Howie deserve better. I don't want to be like that."

She holds up the envelope. "I have to go. *Káthla's* waiting for this." It has a government seal in the corner — same as the one on my dad's pickup.

Out of the corner of my eye, I see a car turn fast into a dirt lane across from the store. It skitters gravel and dust in all directions. Jewel startles. "Oh, *no!*" she gasps, and she takes off running. She dashes out of the parking lot and across the road, then pounds up the driveway, swallowed in the cloud of dust.

What's wrong? I follow as far as the edge of the blacktop. The car skids to a stop right at the door of an unpainted house in an open yard of cheatgrass, the boards burned black by the sun. Now the front door opens, and *Káthla* steps out onto a low stoop a few feet from the front bumper.

A man in a baseball cap and jeans jacket bursts out of the car. He's too far away for me to tell much, except that he is huge. And it is clear from the way he moves that he is angry.

Káthla says something to him as Jewel rushes up, breathing hard. She slips the envelope into her grandmother's hand. *Káthla* stuffs it into her pocket.

The man points at it, then jabs his finger in front of *Káthla*'s face. I can see that he's yelling, even though I can't hear the words. *Káthla* shakes her head firmly.

Suddenly, there's Raymond scuffing along the shoulder of the road up from Shitike Creek. He turns into the drive, looks up toward the house. He stands perfectly still for several seconds. Then he starts running up the driveway.

Jewel shakes her head in a clear signal. *Stop*. Either Raymond doesn't see it or he ignores her.

But the man sees. He whirls around as Raymond comes up from behind. The man's cap is pulled low; I still can't see his face. He crosses his arms and stares at Raymond, who stops with the front of the car between them.

Raymond says something that makes the man raise both arms. *Káthla* quickly steps off the stoop, her hands out. *Calm down*. She stands at Raymond's side and gestures toward the door. *She's inviting that guy in?* Raymond shakes his head at her, and she puts her hand on his arm and nods slightly. It looks like she's telling him that it's okay.

The man takes a step toward the car door, kicks it shut, and then follows them all into the house.

My heart is racing. The bus from the junior high pulls up at the curb with a wheeze of brakes. Jimmy is the first kid to clomp down the stairs, Bill right behind him.

Jimmy grins. "Hey, Kit."

I usually like it when he calls me that, like I'm not some little kid. Right now, I'm too shaky to smile back.

"What're you doing over here?" Bill asks.

"Mom. Letters. Mailbox," I say.

Bill lets me walk with them the two blocks to our house. He goes on about baseball tryouts coming up in a couple of weeks. Pitching, batting, blah, blah, blah.

I keep thinking about that man going into *Káthla*'s house. The whole thing gives me a bad feeling.

⋘⊰◆⊱⋙

The next day, we spend the last half hour before lunch reviewing state capitals for a geography test. Miss Anthony counts us off into pairs, and for once we get to talk to each other during class. Well, sort of. I get stuck with Orin, who never takes anything seriously. Every time I give him a state, he answers with the first thing that pops into his head.

"Idaho," I say.

"Potato," he responds. And it goes like that.

I'm about to ask for another partner when Raymond slinks into the room, dark glasses covering his eyes. There is something crumpled and broken about him.

Orin sees it and shuts right up. And then Dora and Pinky stop talking behind us. Working at her desk, Miss Anthony doesn't notice at first. But the hush that slowly spreads across the room makes her look up.

She stands at her desk. "What's going on here?" she asks Jewel. Jewel has shrunk down into her seat and is silent. Miss Anthony looks more closely at Raymond.

"We do not wear dark glasses in class," she says. "Take them off."

When Raymond doesn't move, Miss Anthony takes a step to the side. The look on her face says she's in no mood for his disrespect. *Do what she says,* I urge him inside my head, *before she reaches for the Bible.*

When Raymond pulls the glasses from his face, Miss Anthony breathes in sharply. "Oh, gracious God," she whispers.

His left eye is battered and raw, a vicious bruise sweeping across his cheek. I'm close enough to see that the short thread of black stitches under his eyebrow oozes a little bit of blood.

I'm thinking that for once Miss Anthony will be sympathetic, until her face hardens. She shakes her head, disgusted. "Another fight?" The noon bell rings in the hall. "Looks like you got the worst of it this time," she says. "Dismissed."

Jewel is outside, sitting alone on one of the logs that separate the parking lot from the playfield. She is hunched over, pulling her sweater tight around her even in the warm sun. She doesn't look up when I sit down, but she moves over a little bit to make room.

"That guy yesterday," I say.

She nods slowly. "He wants us back."

"Your *dad* did that to Raymond?"

"Our dad passed away three years ago," she says, so low I can barely hear her.

My throat catches. "Is that what Pinky meant — 'like last time'?"

Jewel nods. "Yeah. Raymond acted the same way then, and he got put back in third grade with me."

And he's never gotten over it.

Jewel picks at the gravel under her feet. "Walter married mom. And he wants our checks," she says.

The envelope that Jewel handed to her grandmother. People think that Indians get money from the government, but they're wrong. Dad says that the government writes the checks but that it's the tribal members' own money from the sale of timber cut from the forests on the reservation.

"What happened yesterday?"

Jewel shakes her head like it's too hard to explain. Then she says, "*Káthla* wouldn't give him money. They'll just drink it. He started throwing things, shoved her down. And Raymond…" Her voice trails off, but I can picture the rest.

Jewel looks straight at me for the first time. Her eyes are full of tears. "You've got a mom and a dad," she says. She shakes her head again and sighs.

The powerful and angry girl I was afraid of is gone. All I see is a friend with a hurting heart.

"I don't *know* what it's like for you," I tell her. "But I do *care*."

The Capital of Vermont

IT is quiet in the hallway by the time Raymond and Jewel get to school on Friday. Raymond slips into the room ahead of his sister, his battered eye still swollen and raw. He slides into his chair in the next row, two seats ahead of me, and puts his head down on his desk. Miss Anthony gives him a look but doesn't stop writing the last of the states on the board.

The side door at the end of the hall bangs shut. Footsteps slap down the hall, growing louder as the chalk taps and glides across the board. Jewel pauses at the doorway, looking us over. Then she comes in and sits in her desk, to my right.

"You're late," Miss Anthony says to the blackboard. "Take out paper and a pencil."

Jewel glances at my desk. I've already numbered to fifty for the test. She didn't bring anything with her this morning.

I sneak a pencil out of the tray of my desk and pass it off to her down low, then a piece of paper, quickly, before Miss Anthony finishes writing *Wyoming* and turns back around.

"Write the capital of each state," she says.

Then Miss Anthony stares at Raymond's desk. "Not everyone is ready," she observes.

Truman leans forward and pokes Raymond in the back. "*Hey!* She's *lookin'*."

At that, Raymond raises his head from his arms. He scowls back at Truman, and some of the boys start to giggle.

Miss Anthony silences them when she starts to cross the room. All the mice freeze when the coyote stalks. Except for Raymond, who just watches her as she comes.

The kids at the front look straight ahead when she sweeps past. Then they turn to see what will happen this time.

Miss Anthony halts at Raymond's desk, fists on her broad hips. "Where are your work materials?" she asks. "You're so prepared for this test, you don't need paper and pencil?"

Raymond doesn't look at her. He doesn't answer or shake his head or move in any way.

Miss Anthony shifts her weight, crosses her arms. "What is the capital of Vermont?"

Raymond stares straight ahead. His hands lie still on the desk, but the heel of his sneaker jiggles against the floor.

"So. You don't know that one," she says. "How about Washington?"

In any other place, she would sound perfectly reasonable.

"Idaho?"

She has all the time in the world.

"Montana? Oregon?"

He could give her even one and she'd quit. Move on. But he looks like he doesn't even care that she's standing there. Except for his jiggling foot and the sweat that blooms on his neck.

"What *do* you know?" she asks. "Anything?"

A desk leg scrapes beside me, and a form rises up. "Salem," says Jewel quietly. Her voice shakes.

Miss Anthony doesn't even turn. "Not you," she says. "Him."

This is when Raymond moves. He turns to Jewel and shakes his head once. And then he stands too. Miss

Anthony has to step back. She looms over him, but now she's not quite so tall.

Raymond still doesn't look at her. He stares out over our heads.

"You sit down now." Miss Anthony nods to Jewel. "You're not helping him."

Jewel takes a deep breath. "Helena. Boise. Olympia," she says.

In slow motion, Miss Anthony's eyes come up and settle on Jewel. They stay there, hard and cold. I am between her and Jewel now. I hold myself as still as I can.

Miss Anthony points to the door. "Out."

But it's Raymond who goes. While she's fixed on Jewel, he turns away from her and strides up the aisle.

"Get back here!"

Raymond pauses at the doorway, looking down the hall. "Montpelier is the capital of Vermont," he says, and walks through the door.

<hr>

After school, I walk home with Pinky. I feel better being with her. Raymond has plunged himself into big trouble, and I'm sad for him. It's not fair that Miss Anthony just sees the outside part of Raymond, the mean and angry part. She doesn't know that he's hurting inside. Or maybe she doesn't care.

I stop at the top of the trail to her house. "Remember that time we talked about drunks?"

Pinky nods.

"Well, I know about somebody who drinks too much," I say.

It feels good to bring this out in the open. I can't talk to my parents about it—there's nothing they can do. But I need to tell somebody.

She waits.

"Jewel's stepfather."

"Oh yeah," Pinky says. "Mean as a snake, too."

I'm surprised that she's so matter-of-fact. "You know about him?"

"Sure, everybody does."

My heart drops. If people know what Walter's doing but nobody stops him, it's *really* hopeless for Raymond and Jewel.

Pinky shifts her books from one arm to the other. "You know he's not Indian, don't you?"

"*What?*"

"No," she says, "he's a white guy." She makes a face. "He's always hard on those kids. But I think that's the first time he's hit Raymond."

I shake my head. "No wonder he walked out on Miss Anthony."

"What do you mean?"

In the bright afternoon light, I begin to see the dark shadows in Raymond and Jewel's life.

"Maybe he just had enough," I say.

"Enough of what?"

"People beating on him."

<hr />

Spring stretches out toward summer. Every morning when I leave the house, the seam of sunrise that brushes the hills is longer than it was the day before. Birds sing in the poplars all the way to school. But the warmth does not reach inside our classroom.

Jewel serves out her time in Mr. Shanahan's office and then comes back to class. Raymond does not return, and Miss Anthony says nothing about him.

Somehow we get through it. We rip off that last page of the school calendar, with its June rituals of assemblies, projects, cleaning out our desks. The long school year finally comes to an end.

All We've Got

THE temperature is creeping up on eighty degrees in the kitchen when Mom calls the boys to breakfast. I'm at the table already, my bottom scooched forward in the chair to keep the seat from sticking to my sweaty legs.

"Where's Dad?" Bill asks, tipping back his juice.

Mom sets the cereal boxes in the middle of the table. "Down at the Forestry garage getting ready for the parade."

Bill swoops up the Rice Krispies box. "He'll come back for us, right?"

"Of course. The parade won't start for an hour at least."

Independence Day here fires up with a parade, like

all the other places we've lived. But I know from Pinky that the Fourth of July parade at Warm Springs has its own special flavor—flags, drums, beadwork, feathers, bells, horses, pickups, pumper trucks, and heavy machinery. And it's short—one quick swipe around the campus.

We moved here late last summer, so we missed the whole thing. I can't wait to see it. I wish Pinky could be with me, but she is back up at Sidwalter Lookout with her mother. I had almost forgotten how much I hated being all by myself last summer.

"Howie and I dibs the pumper," says Joe. He splashes milk into a bowl overflowing with cereal.

It was a rude surprise that only boys ride in the parade. Because Dad works in Forestry, Bill and Joe get to wear hard hats and wave from the back of a pumper truck or the cab of a bulldozer chained to the long bed of a lowboy. Benson, that lucky duck, gets to whoop the siren of his uncle's patrol car.

I frown over at Mom, but she just smiles.

The spring on the back-door screen boings, and Dad comes in. His short-sleeved shirt is wet and splotchy, and his forehead is damp.

"Everything set?" asks Mom.

Dad nods. "Getting there."

His face is tense. And though he is in a weekend shirt, Dad has on his work pants and boots. The stuff he wears out in the woods or to fires.

"You think it'll go OK?"

Dad sets his glass down and scoops up the cereal bits Joe left strewn over the table. "At least the weather looks good," he says, popping cereal into his mouth.

The weather is one of Dad's big worries in the summer. This morning, the sky above Warm Springs is a clear, uncluttered blue. No sign of clouds that might gather themselves together in the afternoon to become a storm. So it isn't the threat of lightning that wrinkles the skin around his eyes.

Just then, a distant and rapid *pop-pop-pop* from outside. Fireworks. Dad cocks his head toward the window. "*That's* what I'm worried about," he says. "It's so dry out on these hills right now. Wouldn't take much to get a fire going."

Bill and Joe well up out of the basement, all set for parade action in their new Forestry T-shirts. I don't even get one of those—just a towel to dry the rest of the dishes Mom is washing. They sweep out of the door after Dad, piling into the station wagon. Next time I see them, they'll be sitting up on the machinery, waving like goofy homecoming royalty.

By the time the kitchen is clean, I can hear noises

in the distance. The parade must be forming up in the parking lot at McKenzie's store. Mom takes pity on me and waves me outside. I grab a spot at the curb and watch the parade come up the street.

A VFW color guard marches with the flags—the Stars and Stripes and the deep blue and gold of the Confederated Tribes. We all stand up, hands on hearts, as they pass. Then we sit back down for the dignitaries. The chiefs of the three tribes—Warm Springs, Wasco, and Paiute—ride on horseback wearing their regalia. The tribal council chairman waves from the back seat of a convertible.

Then comes a rolling line of cars and pickups covered in brightly colored blankets, people riding on the hoods and the truck beds. Whole families have brought out their best beadwork and baskets to display. I see Geraldine and Dora from my class wearing wing dresses, their hair braided and tied with otter fur.

"Hey, Kitty!" They wave hard at me. Dora holds a little girl close to her side on the hood of the car, her arm tight around her waist. Makes me think of Tela for a sad moment. I'll bet she would have loved this parade.

Finally, the big rigs pass by. I see Joe on the back of the pumper with Howie, both in hard hats that keep slipping down over their eyes. Behind them, Bill smirks at me from high on the seat of a bulldozer. The boys toss out handfuls of bubblegum to the crowd lining the street.

"Kitty!" Howie shouts. "For you!" He swings his arm way back and sprays several pieces right at my feet. I give him back a big smile.

When the parade ends, there will be a picnic down at the ball fields, and an afternoon of games. That means bottles of pop glistening in tubs of ice. Mom usually forbids pop, but she's making an exception for this special occasion. Pinky promised me that it's all free. I sure do miss her.

I follow the crowd down the hill, walking on the shoulder of the road. The ball fields have been transformed into one giant festival. It seems like everybody on the reservation must have come. It doesn't feel strange anymore that most of the people are Indian, and I realize how many faces I know. Kids from school and grown-ups, too, from the boys' baseball games and Friday night movies up at the school. Mr. Walsey from the dining hall stands at a giant barbecue grill, calling out greetings and offering hot dogs and hamburgers.

I make a beeline for the icy tubs of pop, working my way through the thirsty mob. I bend down to fish out a bottle, but somebody hands me one already opened. It's Jewel, popping off the cap of another bottle with an opener tied onto the tub handle.

"Hi," she says. But something isn't right. She looks anxious.

We move into the shade of the home bleachers. "How are you?" I ask. "I haven't seen you since school got out."

Jewel takes a sip of her pop. It is still and hot, even here in the shade. Her hand glistens with condensation from the cold bottle. "He's gone right now."

"Your stepfather?"

Jewel nods.

"Well, that's a good thing, huh?" I ask.

She shrugs. "He takes off...and then he shows up again. We never know when or where."

"What about your mom?" I ask her. Mothers are supposed to protect their children.

Jewel doesn't speak for a second. Then she looks at me with that hard face I haven't seen in ages.

"She gave up a long time ago. *Káthla* is all we've got."

I hate that she's so helpless. "Can't your grandma tell somebody?"

"Like who?" she says, shaking her head. "The tribal cops can't touch him. And" — Jewel looks away — "the sheriff's office...they're all white. They won't do a thing."

Fireworks

SUDDENLY, the siren on the concrete roof of Fire Control winds up. Men race for their cars and pickups.

Bill waves his arms at me from the other side of the field. Sweat glistens on his bare forehead. The fire call must have come in right when the boys hopped off the equipment at the parade's end.

"I have to go," I tell Jewel. "Something's up."

Bill has taken off running, Joe right behind him. I follow them to the shortcut up the hill behind the jail. I scoot around the side of the house as the boys bang through the screen door.

Mom is already making sandwiches. She has the lunch meat on the counter and the waxed paper in her hand. Every time Dad goes out on a fire, she sends food.

Sometimes he is gone a couple of hours, sometimes a couple of days. We just never know.

"Would you find some fruit?" Mom shouts over the siren noise that invades the kitchen. "Dad has to get going."

I scoop apples out of the refrigerator. "Where's the fire?"

The siren winds down and then builds back up. "Somewhere up in the mountains. Lightning," Mom says. She works around me, filling Dad's canteen at the tap, bagging cookies, folding a paper towel for a napkin.

By the time we're done, Dad is ready to go. Now he's wearing a woods shirt with his work pants and boots.

"Stay by the radio," he tells Mom, holding the screen open with his boot. "I may need you to relay messages."

Dad runs to the truck and is gone. Then a pickup just like his speeds down the street. A couple of seconds later, a tribal police car with its lights flashing. All headed down to Fire Control below the hill.

⟜⟜⟜HOH⟞⟞⟞

All afternoon and into the evening, the radio in the hall is alive with voices. Mrs. Quempts checks in from the Shitike Butte lookout tower, then Mrs. Wesley on

Sidwalter where Pinky is, and Mrs. Suppah on Eagle. The gravelly voice of Mr. Wirt down in the dispatch center threads the reports together, and slowly I learn the details. Lightning from a big storm by Mount Jefferson sparked the first plumes of smoke that quickly raged into a thick column boiling up over the foothills, visible from all three lookout towers. In a matter of hours, the fire grew into the largest of the season. And the fire crews have not yet reached it on the ground.

Dad checks in on the radio in his pickup, way out on Tenino Road, and then Mom makes us come to the table. She turns up the volume so that we can still listen. We eat supper beneath the babble of the airwaves.

"Let's go watch the fireworks later," Mom says. "We can see them from right behind the jail. We won't be far away in case —"

Screeching static erupts out of the radio, loud even in the kitchen. Lightning breaks up the transmission. "Mobile One. This is Sidwalter. Come in." Mrs. Wesley is calling Dad in his pickup.

"This is Mobile One — go ahead, Sidwalter," he says, steady and calm, though he must be hurtling down that gravel road as fast as he can get the truck to go.

"We've got dozens of strikes flaming up." Even through the airwaves, we can hear the chaos that enfolds

Mrs. Wesley way out in the tower. Thunder booms and sets the static ablaze.

"Ten-four, Sidwalter," my dad replies. "A crew's on the way."

I glance over at Mom. She has stopped in midbite, listening hard, her face still. "Mom?"

"They'll be OK, honey," she says, and hurries out of the kitchen.

We follow her, crowding around the radio. I settle onto the floor, leaning up against the wall. We're still there in the hall when dusk fades to darkness outside. Fireworks start rattling the bathroom window, and sparkles of light from down at the ball fields reflect off the mirror.

"We'll see them next year," Bill says.

"Hey there, sleepyhead," Mom greets me as I walk into the kitchen in the morning. She is making a shopping list, and recipes are spread all over the kitchen table.

"Where's Dad?" I ask.

"Out in Seekseequa Canyon. He called in about an hour ago and said they were having a tough time getting a line around the fire."

"It's that big?"

"They'll get it under control," she says.

I can tell Mom knows I'm worried, because she changes the subject. "I've got to go to town this morning—groceries and the fabric store. You want to come?"

I can't think of anything more boring, but my options are limited. "OK. Can we stop by the library?" That will make it bearable.

Mom finds what she needs right away, so we're done in no time and ready to head for home after a quick stop at the library. She drops me off outside the building.

"Grab your books," she says, then points to the gas pumps across the street. "I'll meet you over at the Standard station. The tank's about empty."

When I pull open the heavy wooden door, I see Cathy Watson leaning on the broad counter while the librarian checks out her stack of books. Once that new girl, Linda, showed up at church last fall, Cathy and the other girls ignored me. Not that I wanted to go to their birthday parties or join Campfire Girls, but it still hurts that in Sunday school every week they act like I'm not even there.

I slide behind Cathy, hoping she won't notice. But she's gathering up her books when I come back to the counter with my own pile.

"You have your card?" the librarian asks me.

That makes Cathy look up. She gives me a polite

smile, but there's no friendship in it. She turns, says thank you to the librarian, and pushes open the door.

On the way back home, by my own breezy window in the front seat, I replay what I wish Cathy had said. "Kitty, it's really great to see you!" Or "Let's get our moms to take us to the movies." I'm never going to hear anything like that.

The highway stretches up the hill away from Madras toward one of my favorite views, a long flat plain of mint fields and alfalfa reaching far out toward the mountains. When we crest the hill, I see that off in the distance, storm clouds tower over Mount Jefferson, their flat undersides black. But they aren't what scares me. It's the monster column of yellow-gray smoke boiling over the rugged slopes above Seekseequa Canyon. No wonder the firefighters are having trouble getting a line around the fire.

"Uh-oh," Mom says. "That's not good."

I can't look at all that smoke. I slap my hands over my eyes and put my head down.

"It's OK, honey," she says.

I keep my chin pressed to my chest. "Dad's out there. "

Mom pats my leg, then puts her hand back on the wheel.

It is now a long ride home. I don't look up until the road dips down below the rimrock. I count the curves down the long canyon until the pavement turns west, crosses the Deschutes River, and runs safely straight again toward Warm Springs.

When I get out of the car in our driveway, a stiff breeze fans dust over the flowers at the border of the yard. Bill sticks his head out the back door. "Mom!" he yells. "It's Dad—phone!"

Mom hurries in, pointing at the station wagon as she goes. Bill scowls barefoot out to the car, throws open the tailgate, and hefts a loaded grocery bag in each arm. "Shut it," he commands, turning back to the house.

I have to reach up on tiptoe to grab the handle and practically swing with my feet off the ground to pull down the heavy car door. The wind has picked up—dust and gravel now swirl around my legs. I heave the tailgate shut and sprint for the house.

Joe sits at the kitchen table, the carcass of a peanut butter sandwich on his plate. "Somebody died," he says.

"*What?*"

"Out at the fire. A bulldozer rolled over, and a guy got squished."

"Joe! Cut it out!" I don't want to imagine that stuff.

"Busted his head wide open," he says.

I slug him on the arm and rush out of the kitchen. Mom is still at the phone in the hall, saying, "Oh, Bud, that's horrible."

I slip out to the sun porch and close the door so I don't have to hear any more. I slump down on the padded bench built into the wall and hug the pillow covered with Grandma's old curtains. Through the bank of windows, I can see the wind slashing at the tall poplars down the street. The sky is clouded over, and it feels heavy and dark.

The door from the living room opens. "You OK?" asks Bill. He comes and sits down next to me, leans back against the wall, and pulls up his knees. "Joe's a big dope. Nobody's dead."

"Yeah?"

"Course not. A guy got hurt, but his head isn't busted."

"Will he be OK?" I ask into the pillow.

"Yeah. They took him to the hospital in Prineville. Dad called from there."

It must have been bad if Dad left the fire to go with him.

A low rumble, quiet and far away at first, keeps coming and rolls over the house. The first drops of rain clatter against the porch as Mom calls for Bill to help her close windows. In seconds, every pane of glass is dripping.

Bottom of the fifth

WHEN the storm passes off to the east, I open the back door. Cool air blows in through the screen, clearing out the moist heat trapped in the house. Maybe the rain will help with the fire, I think hopefully.

A couple of hours later, I'm sitting on the back step reading when I hear Bill and Joe on their way home from baseball practice. The sound of their arguing reaches me even before I can see them. The sun is fully back and hot, the dust dried and puffing up under their feet as they scuff through the gravel in the driveway.

"Goofus here couldn't catch a grounder if it was handed to him." Bill pounds the dust out of his glove on the side of the house, storms inside, and slams the screen door behind him.

Joe sits down beside me. Both knees are scraped raw below the fringe of his cutoffs. He must have been playing the far outfield, which is cluttered with rocks and thorny cheatgrass.

"What's up?" I ask.

"Bill's mad 'cause he's not pitching tonight."

"How come?"

"Sherf put him on third base," Joe says. "Raymond showed up today."

"He *did?*" Raymond hasn't played all summer, and I've been wondering where he was.

Joe wipes a drip of blood off his knee with his finger. "Yep."

Mom calls us in to supper. There's still no word from Dad, so she covers a plate in waxed paper and puts it back in the refrigerator.

<hr />

The game is way out in Metolius, a long drive into the heart of Madras, then out the back road along the west side of the valley. The neat lawns in town thin out to a scattering of junkyards and feedlots, then there's nothing but a few straight miles of sagebrush until we get to the next water tower. Metolius is smaller than Madras, about the size of Warm Springs. The ball field spreads out behind the grade school on the far side of town.

As soon as Mom stops, Joe dashes out of the car and onto the field. She leaves the engine running.

"Kitty," she says, "I've got to go into Madras for a quick meeting at the church. I'll be back before the game's over."

Bill waits for me as she drives away. I know just from looking at him that he has something to tell me but isn't sure how to say it.

"What?" I ask.

He glances around quickly. "I wouldn't say anything if Mom was still here. But keep your eyes open tonight."

"How come?"

"There's this guy who shows up at games when we play off the reservation. Sometimes he says stuff." He walks me over to the bleachers.

"Like what?" I ask.

Bill sighs. "Look, just things that can be really... ugly. I want you to be ready." And he trots over to the bench to join his team.

I take my book and find a spot at the edge of the bleachers right behind the backstop. Out of the way of batting practice and foul balls and any crazy, mean people. From here, I have a clear view of the Metolius crowd. They look pretty normal — and harmless.

Sherf parks his battered pickup beside the bleachers

and pulls a canvas bag of balls and bats out of the truck bed. Then Raymond, with his glove, slides out on the passenger side.

He follows the coach up to the backstop and hesitates. There's a big man in a John Deere cap leaning against the fence. The man starts to say something, but Raymond pushes past him. The man curls his fingers into the chainlink fence and watches Raymond jog onto the field.

There's still no score in the bottom of the fifth. When Metolius comes up to bat, the crowd gets quiet. The big red-haired guy who plays left field hefts a bat across his shoulder and then pounds it on the plate.

The umpire signals to Raymond, who nods once at the batter and throws. The kid doesn't even twitch until the ball thunks into Jimmy's glove. And then he glances down at Jimmy like, *Where'd that come from?*

"Strike one!"

Jimmy tosses the ball back to Raymond. The red-haired kid takes a couple of swings and waits, bat poised.

Another shot. Another *thwack!* "Strike two!"

A buzz sweeps through the crowd on the Metolius side, like a hive of angry bees.

"Hey, ump!" the man behind the backstop yells,

right in the umpire's ear. "Get your eyes checked!" He turns to the side and plunks a long stream of brown tobacco spit into the dirt.

Raymond hides the ball in his glove, chin to his chest, and stands still on the mound.

"Throw that thing!" hollers the man, dropping his arms from the fence. "C'mon, Chief!"

That's what Bill was talking about. That is ugly.

Raymond lifts his head slowly, but he doesn't wind up. His eyes dark under his baseball cap, he glares at the man. I've seen him when he's mad, but this is something more. Something different.

Raymond winds up and throws another straight shot. This time, the batter snags a corner of the ball and sends a hard grounder right back at the mound. Raymond scoops it up and cocks his arm as the boy flings the bat and pounds toward first. He is only about halfway up the line when Raymond lets loose.

But he doesn't throw to Dawson, who's got his foot on first base and glove out. Raymond throws right at the runner like he is sighting down the barrel of a gun. I shudder when the ball slams into the boy's ankle and he goes down screaming.

The Metolius fans rise as one as their team boils off the bench, everyone yelling. The coaches and players swarm the screeching boy. Between their legs, I see one black heel pounding a crater in the dirt. I'm horrified that Raymond would do something so terrible.

Out on the field, the Warm Springs players stand in stunned silence. All but Raymond, who turns and walks off the mound. He takes off his glove and drops it into Sherf's hands right in front of where I'm sitting.

"Nobody calls me Chief," he says.

All the Way Back to
the Black Eye

SHERF and the umpire stand between Raymond and
the angry Metolius fans pressing in on home plate. The
man who was yelling at Raymond has vanished in the
confusion.

Bill grabs Joe and waves me off the bleachers. I
scramble down and run after them as Mom pulls up in
the station wagon.

She rolls down the window. "Game over already?"

"Raymond whacked a kid with the ball," Joe says.
"On purpose."

Mom shakes her head, but she doesn't look
surprised.

We ride in silence most of the way home. My heart

is still pounding and my hands are sweaty. I keep going over what would make Raymond do such a hideous thing. Then somehow I know. *That was Raymond's step-father at the backstop.*

Bill says, "Just as well that Dad missed the game. Raymond wrecked it for us."

Mom's eyes meet his in the rearview mirror. "He had no reason to do something like that," she says.

Maybe he did.

Bill looks at me. I must have said it out loud.

"Didn't you see that man yelling at Raymond?" I ask.

"Yeah. That's the guy I was telling you about."

We turn off the highway at the gas station and take the back way past McKenzie's. Sure enough, Dad's pickup is parked where I want it to be — in our driveway.

"Hi, troops," Dad says as we fill up the kitchen. He's sitting at the table with the plate of food Mom left. He looks tired, and his shirt and pants are grimy. But his face is clean. He's been here long enough to wash up. Then I see the clean socks on his feet. I guess he won't be home for long. It must be bad out there.

Mom doesn't even have to ask, she just puts her hand on his shoulder.

Dad shakes his head. "It's not looking so good." Then he says, "You kids go brush your teeth. I'll come say good night before I leave." He wants us out of the kitchen so they can talk.

Bill catches my eye and cocks his chin toward the hall, pulling Joe through the doorway by his shirt.

"What do you think is going on?" I ask. The voices in the kitchen are low now.

"Sherf was talking about the fire tonight before the game," Bill says. "They can't get a line around it. Until they do, nothing can stop it."

The living room window is dark. It's almost nine, past our bedtimes. Dad appears in the doorway.

"Do not worry about this," he says gently.

"What are you going to do?" Joe asks.

"We're going back out there, we're getting a line around that beast, and we're saving the timber." It's what he always says about forest fires.

"Do you have to go now?" I ask.

He nods. "'Fraid so, honey. They need me at fire camp."

I throw my arms around his waist. Dad hugs me close, and I'm wrapped in the smell of him—aftershave, pipe tobacco, forest, and smoke.

I don't want him to leave. I want him here. I want to tell him about Raymond—he'll know what to do. But in the next minute he's gone out the door and back to the fire.

The phone rings as I walk through the dark hall to my room. It's late for someone to be calling. If something's happened, why didn't it come over the radio?

I'm closest, so I pick it up. "Hello?"

"Raymond's been arrested for assault!" It's Jimmy, his voice breathless. In a quick tumble of words, he tells me. A sheriff's deputy roared up right after we left. Siren, lights, and everything. He grabbed Raymond and put him in handcuffs and pushed him down into the back seat of the patrol car. The whole thing took only seconds, and then Raymond was gone.

"Gotta go," Jimmy says. "Tell Bill he's back on the mound." And he hangs up.

I can't believe it. Raymond's in super-deep trouble, and somebody needs to know the whole story. He picked an innocent target, but Raymond has good reason to want to hurt somebody.

When I walk back into the living room, Mom asks, "Who was that?" Then she looks more closely at me. "Kitty...what's wrong?" She takes my hand and gently pulls me over to the couch.

I slump down. "Bill gets to pitch." He looks surprised. I'm glad for him, but this isn't the way it should happen.

I take a deep breath and tell her everything—the handcuffs, the yelling at the game, all the way back to the black eye. All I know about how Walter treats Raymond and Jewel. Everything I've kept inside because I didn't know what else to do.

"Those poor kids," Mom says. "I had no idea that was going on. Why didn't you say something?"

I shake my head. "I just—" I'm afraid I'm going to cry. "I didn't think it would do any good."

Mom is quiet for a few moments. Then she puts both hands on my shoulders. "Honey, the police need to know about Raymond and his stepfather."

"*No.*" I jerk back. "I can't talk to them!"

"You know this is important." Mom holds me firmly, looks in my eyes. "You have to tell them what you saw."

No Defense

THERE is no arguing with Mom about something like this. She makes some calls in the morning, and right after breakfast, she and I head into Madras. The Jefferson County sheriff's office is right in the middle of town. Mom parks the car between two green and white cruisers.

I find a seat in the lobby while Mom talks to the officer behind the counter. I sit on the backs of my hands, keeping my legs off the sweaty plastic.

Mom comes back and sits down with me. "It will be a couple of minutes," she says. "They're waiting for the tribal police."

My stomach pulls tighter. "How many people do I have to talk to?"

I can tell she's trying to look reassuring, but it doesn't help. "Raymond's a tribal member and a juvenile. The Warm Springs police need to be involved."

It's not going to make any difference. Jewel said there's nothing they can do.

I distract myself by looking around at the knots of people in the quiet room. Some of them also have big troubles or they wouldn't be here.

Káthla and Jewel come through the glass doors. Jewel helps her grandmother ease into a chair and then sets a paper sack down next to her. Maybe they've brought Raymond clean clothes or something to eat. Jewel goes up to the counter and stands for a while before the officer looks up. They talk briefly, then the officer points to the chairs and she sits back down.

In the meantime, Mom goes over to *Káthla*. "It's nice to see you again, Bessie." She sits with her hand on the back of *Káthla*'s chair. Now and then, *Káthla* puts a handkerchief up to her eyes as they talk.

I'm wondering if I should go too, when Jewel sees me. I wave, and she comes and sits down.

"We're going away," she says quietly. "Soon as we can get Raymond out of here."

"Where?"

"The mountains. *Káthla* says he's getting worse."

"Raymond?" I ask, then instantly feel stupid when I see the hurt in her face.

Jewel's eyes fill with tears, but she doesn't cry. "No," she whispers. *"Him."*

We sit in silence for a few moments.

"The police can help you," I say finally. "I'm going to tell them about Walter…"

Jewel grabs the arm of my chair and stares me in the eye. She looks fierce and scared. "You can't say anything," she says. "If he finds out, he'll come right after us."

"If I tell them what Walter's done, he'll go to jail," I insist. "Then you'll be safe."

Desperation tightens Jewel's face. "You don't get it," she says, her voice hard and low. "They will *not* listen to *you*." Tears glisten on her lashes. She wipes them away. *"Káthla* says they can't hold Raymond any longer. He's just a kid. He's getting released this morning, and she'll take us up to the huckleberry fields. Walter won't be able to find us there." Then she stands. *"Please,"* she says. "Do not tell *anybody*." She walks across the room and slumps down in her chair.

A few minutes later, an officer opens a door and calls out Raymond's name. Jewel helps *Káthla* get up, and Mom hands her the sack. Jewel clasps her grandmother's arm, and together they walk across the lobby.

The glass doors open again, and an Indian police-man steps inside. It's the guy Joe talked to on the way to baseball practice last summer. Mr. Wewa. In his crisp uniform, he looks like he belongs here. But when he goes up to the counter, the officer makes him wait before he looks up. Then they talk briefly.

Mom walks over and introduces herself. Then she beckons to me. "Mr. Wewa," she says, "this is my daughter, Kitty."

Grownups don't usually shake hands with me, but he reaches out his hand, and his grip is solemn and soft. "You're doing the right thing," Mr. Wewa says.

A gray metal door opens and a deputy comes out. He holds a clipboard in his hand, a sheaf of pages flipped over. "Kitty Schlick," he calls out.

"All right," Mom says. "Here you go."

"You're not coming with me?" I can't keep the panic out of my voice.

"They asked me to wait out here." Mom smiles like she's trying to convince me. "I said it was OK."

"I'll be there too," Mr. Wewa says. He gestures for me to follow, and I make myself walk with him through the metal door.

The deputy leads us down a hall and into a small office. He points me to a chair, and we all sit around a table. He flips to a sheet that looks like a blank form. He clicks open his pen, then gives me what he must think is a friendly smile.

"How old are you?" he asks.

"Eleven. I'll be twelve in two weeks."

The deputy scribbles for a second, then says, "Your mom says you have information about the Danzuka case."

I just sit there. Jewel's fear weighs me down.

"Young lady," the officer says, his voice impatient, "what did you want to tell us?"

Mr. Wewa encourages me with a nod.

"Something happened at the game," I say. "To Raymond, before he threw the ball at that kid."

I tell them about Walter standing behind the backstop yelling mean things at Raymond. And more — about the beating and the government check and everything I know about what he's done to Raymond and Jewel. I feel horrible for telling, but they have to realize how bad things are. "You've got the wrong guy in jail," I say at the end.

The deputy doesn't write anything down. He just looks at me, frowning.

"Is that it?" he asks. "He called Raymond 'Chief'?"

I'm not sure what he means. "Yes, but there's all

the rest, too." I feel stupid. It's clear that he doesn't believe me.

The deputy turns to Mr. Wewa. "A guy calls the boy 'Chief,' and he *attacks* a kid with a baseball?"

"It's an insult," Mr. Wewa says. "And possibly a form of abuse."

"Well, it's no defense," the deputy says, and he slaps all the pages back to the front of the clipboard.

I'm stunned. I told them everything I knew about Walter, even after Jewel begged me to stay quiet. And they're not going to do a thing to him.

"You can go," the deputy says.

My hands are shaking. I hold my breath and will myself not to cry. Not here, not in front of him.

Mr. Wewa walks me out into the hall. "Thank you for coming up here." His voice sounds so kind.

"*Káthla* and Jewel are really scared of him," I blurt. "They don't feel safe in their own house."

Mr. Wewa's face is serious. "Is there something you haven't told us?"

Jewel was right about the police. Saying any more won't make one bit of difference. And it could make things a whole lot worse if somehow Walter found out.

Mr. Wewa is watching my face. I don't trust my voice, so I simply shake my head.

I have just lied to a policeman.

"Well, if you hear anything," he says, "please ask your mother to call me."

I nod and get myself out of that hallway as fast as I can.

Rock the Culvert

THE telephone is my alarm clock in the morning. Mom answers and says, "Sure, Kitty's up. Just a sec."

She pokes her head in my door. "Pinky is back from the lookout. She wants you to come over."

And that lifts some of the gloom I've carried ever since I left the police station yesterday. I dash through breakfast and out into the morning. The air is cooler than it has been—dry and fresh. No clouds disturb the deep blue overhead. A perfect day now that Pinky is home.

She waits for me on the steps of her house right across the road from the bottom of the dusty trail.

"Hey—I thought you'd never get back!" I tell her, opening the gate.

"Mom sent me home from Sidwalter 'cause she's nervous about that fire and didn't want to have to worry about me, too."

I know her dad is out on the fire with my dad. "So, who's staying with you?" I ask.

She rolls her eyes. "Pete. You don't want to come in."

Pete is Pinky's older brother, the one who works in the Roads Department maintenance yard next door. He is way past the age when you have to live at home, but he does.

"Pete was out on the fire line with the bulldozer until late," she says, standing up. "He's asleep."

She leans in close and lowers her voice. "You wanna go rock the culvert?"

"Huh?"

"C'mere." Pinky tugs me over to her back fence and points down into the maintenance yard, where the Roads Department keeps the bulldozers and road graders and dump trucks.

I can't see what she's so excited about. "Yeah, so?"

Then I follow her patient finger. In the corner that backs up to Shitike Creek, something glints in the sun. Through the bushes, I finally make out what looks like a giant open can of peas on its side. It's a culvert, ready to be hauled off into the woods and installed under some new logging road.

I don't know what Pinky has in mind. I'm pretty sure that our moms would kill us for going into that yard. But I bet it'll be fun.

The gate's open. The fire crews drove the lowboys loaded with bulldozers through here on their way out to the fire. Now nobody is around. "All clear," Pinky says, and leads me down the driveway and through the gate.

The Roads yard is cluttered with heavy machinery, mostly broken down and rusted. All the good stuff is out at work on the fire.

I follow Pinky as she threads her way across the yard to where the culvert rests up against the fence. She gestures for me to stand beside her inside the echoing metal tunnel. It is barely big enough for me to stand up straight.

"Go!" she shouts.

Pinky stretches her arms out toward the upward-curving ribs of the culvert, then throws her weight against the wall. I quickly get it that I've got to move with her, that we have to pump back and forth, pushing on each side, just like getting a swing into the air.

We hit the cold metal together, then turn and push the other side. If we can get the right rhythm going, we can rock the culvert — maybe even roll the whole thing all the way over.

It takes some sweaty teamwork before the culvert moves even slightly. But it slowly begins to rock. I'm on the inside with my eyes closed, and with every push, I feel the culvert roll a little bit more.

And then Pinky goes, "Uh-oh."

"What in the heck do you think you're doing?"

I open my eyes to see that Pinky has turned to stone. Her brother, Pete, has appeared without a sound. He stands on the gravel, his arms crossed.

"Get on out of there," he orders.

Pinky steps out from the shadows, pulling me with her. Then she grasps my arms and edges in behind me.

"*Answer* me," he says. "What are you two doing down here?"

Pinky doesn't speak.

"We know it was dumb," I blurt. I don't know if I'm more scared of him or more ashamed about getting caught.

"You," he says. "Go home." And then to Pinky, "In the house."

I'm afraid not to do what he says. Without a word, Pinky and I step around him. As we scoot back up the hill toward the gate, I hear his boots crunch the gravel behind us.

"You wanna come home with me?" I whisper.

"He barks, but he doesn't bite."

Pinky ducks into her yard ahead of Pete, and I hurry on home, afraid the phone will ring before I can get there.

This Would Be the Time

I spend the whole afternoon waiting for Pete to call and tell on us. But the waiting is as bad as any trouble that's going to come, so I escape outside with my book.

It's not so hot in the shade of the locust tree, but out in the sun the heat shimmers. The green campus is quiet, and so are the basketball court and the swings at the far end. Just the steady *tick-tick-tick* of the big sprinklers out on the grass. Now and then a car or truck passes on the street, raising dust.

I'm on the last few pages when Dad's truck wheels into the driveway. He waves at me from the cab, and I get up to help him haul his gear out of the back.

"Hi, honey," he says, giving me a sweaty, smoky hug.

"Is the fire out?"

Dad kisses the top of my head. "Pretty near, if the line and the weather hold."

Joe bursts out the back door, Mom close behind. Joe and I lug the fire gear down to the basement by the washer. Mom will sort through it later.

"The mop-up will go on for a couple of days, but it looks good out there," Dad's saying as I come back upstairs.

"What happened to the guy on the bulldozer?" I ask.

Dad puts his arm around my waist. "He's in the hospital. The cage saved him when it rolled over. Went real fast, and he didn't get thrown out. Everybody was very lucky this time."

"Did the bulldozer get burned up?" Joe asks.

Dad shakes his head. "You should see it—what a mess. They hauled it down to the Roads yard."

I head back outside but stop short when he says, "I gotta find out if Pete thinks we can salvage it."

Pete will be happy to tell him. And then some.

<hr>

After supper, Mom opens all the doors and windows, funneling the cooling breeze from outside. She and Dad sit on the front steps with tea. Inside, on the padded bench on the porch, I start on my next library book. I can hear the low hum of their voices through the screen.

My eyes are on the book, but my mind goes back to Raymond. I used to be afraid of him. Now I picture him in a cold jail cell with murderers. He must have been really scared.

I couldn't say anything to Mom when I got out of that deputy's office at the police station. And she didn't press me. She just hugged me, and then we came home.

I tried to help, but it didn't work. And I'm not saying anything else about it. To anyone.

Bill and Joe come in as it is getting dark. Practice must have run late. Through the house, I hear the the screen door creak and the wood banging against the doorframe. Bill comes out onto the porch, dust all over his jeans. He rubs an apple on his T-shirt, then takes a big bite. "Mom and Dad?" he asks.

I point to the open front door without looking up from my book. "On the steps."

Bill flops down beside me. He radiates heat and sweat.

"How'd it go?" I ask, scooching away from his tangy smell.

"We had some pretty great pitching, if I do say so myself."

"Is this for good?"

Bill shrugs. "Maybe. Sherf didn't say a thing about Raymond. Or about the Metolius game."

Joe comes out on the porch, mud splatters on his bare legs. Outfield practice again. Then Mom walks in dangling an empty cup, Dad behind her.

"Bath time," she says to Joe, and points into the house. "You first." She follows him through the doorway to the living room.

Dad settles down on the empty seat. "Mr. Wewa came to see me today," he says. He pulls his pipe out of his pocket and holds it unlit between his teeth.

"He told you?" I ask, keeping my eyes on my book.

"Yep. That must have been hard for you."

I really don't want to talk about this. But Dad doesn't sound like he's in a hurry. I have to say something or he'll keep coming back to it.

"Raymond's going back to jail."

Dad shakes his head. "Not necessarily. His grandmother took him home, and Mr. Wewa thinks he can work something out."

I know that this would be the time to speak up, to tell him that the family has gone into hiding. However, I didn't tell Mr. Wewa the truth yesterday, and now I can't tell Dad, either. So I keep my mouth shut.

Dad sucks air gently through the empty bowl of the pipe. We sit in the cool quiet as the porch grows shadows. Then he says, "I got a call from Pete."

Yikes. I'd thought maybe I had escaped.

"You and Pinky—"

"We didn't mean to!"

Bill lets out a disgusted snort. *Never admit anything!*

"What?" Dad cocks his head.

"The culvert. He told you, right?"

Bill slaps his hand hard on the cushion. *Shut up already.*

Dad takes the pipe out of his mouth. "No," he says in a tone that means, *But you're going to.*

"We were only playing." So dumb. I can almost feel Bill rolling his eyes beside me.

"Playing *where?*" Dad asks, even though he knows. I gave it up when I said "culvert." This is what parents do—they make you say it. One minute they feel sorry for you; the next, they sweat you under hot lights.

I spill it out in one long breath. "We were playing in the culvert at the Roads yard." *There.*

Dad sits up straight. I wither down into the bench cushions.

"Are you supposed to go inside the Roads yard?" he asks in that quiet way parents get when they're mad.

"No," I say to my knees.

"*Ever?*" The disappointment in his voice makes my throat tight.

"No."

Beside me, Bill moves his arm a fraction, touching

my shoulder. *You're an idiot, but I'm here.* That pushes me over the edge, and I put my hands up to my face and cry hard. "I'm sorry, Dad," I blubber. "I know it was wrong."

He puffs out a big breath, leans back against the cushion, and puts his arm around my shoulders. "It's so dangerous down there. You girls have no idea."

Mom steps out onto the porch. "Bill, your turn for the tub," she says. Then she hesitates. "Everything all right?"

Please don't tell her, I beg Dad inside my head. *I'll never do it again.*

"Just fine," he says. "We'll be along in a second."

Bill gets right up and goes with her. Later, he'll tell me what a stupid dope I am, but he's on my side for now.

Dad sucks on the pipe and keeps his arm around my shoulders. I blow out a couple of times to stop crying.

"You know that work areas are off-limits," he says.

"Yes."

"And you know why."

I nod. Of course I do. "They're dangerous places for kids, and people need to work there."

"OK." He takes his pipe out of his mouth and kisses the top of my head. "Let's leave it at that."

It is now almost dark on the porch. Through the

windows, I can barely make out the poplars waving in the evening breeze. That's the only sound that comes through the screen door.

"Pete called to ask if you could go back up to the lookout with Pinky," Dad says.

"He didn't tell you about the culvert?"

"Nope." I can feel him smiling. "You would've gotten clean away." He stretches out his arms and yawns. "Now that the fire's under control, it's safe for Pinky to go back up there. Mrs. Wesley radioed in to see if he'd bring her. She thought you might want to spend a couple of days up at Sidwalter to keep her company."

"Can I?"

Dad stands up, pulling me to my feet. "It's already cleared with Mom," he says. "Pete's picking you up in the morning."

Welcome to Sidwalter

THE journey to Sidwalter Lookout begins at the highway that links Warm Springs to the outside world. To the north and west is Portland — up the steep, winding canyon, out across the broad flat of sagebrush and juniper, and then into the deep woods at HeHe Butte. Up on top, the snow-crested heads of the Cascades spread to the south and the grizzled brown Mutton Mountains to the north. The city sprawls on the other side of the mountains, a hundred miles and two long hours away.

If you turn right at the main entrance to Warm Springs, you go south and east — off the reservation at the Deschutes River, up another twisted canyon grade, then across the wide-open mix of mint and scablands to Madras, Prineville, Redmond, or Bend. Go straight at the stop sign, and you end up on the hot, dusty road to Simnasho, and if you go far enough, the Columbia River. Whichever way you go, the road climbs to higher ground.

Pete rumbles over the cattle guard, pauses at the stop sign, and cranks the steering wheel hard to the left. In seconds, we shoot past the boys' dorm, the school and its playground, the curved row of teacher houses at the edge of the community. Pete works the gears as we begin the long climb to the top of the canyon. He has to work around Pinky's short legs. She moves them over closer to me, leaning to get away from his elbow.

Our stuff is behind us in the pickup bed, covered with a tarp and tied down to keep the dust out of the sleeping bags and knapsacks. Mom tucked a sack of peaches for Mrs. Wesley under the tarp. She told me to be good, have fun, and do what Mrs. Wesley tells me. Then she waved goodbye, never letting on that she knew anything about the culvert.

Even in the early morning, the air blasting through the open windows is hot. Pressed against the door, I lean my elbow into the wind and hold my hair out of my face. The flat open plain, dotted with sagebrush and deep green junipers, is beautiful in a lonely kind of way. Unexpectedly, I'm filled with happiness. It strikes me how much this landscape feels like home.

Pinky leans away from her silent brother and says

behind her hand, "He's mad that he has to use his day off to take us." She smiles, careful not to let him see.

"How far is it?" I ask her. I've never been to any of the lookouts. The only one I've seen is the long-legged spire that sits on the bald knob of Eagle Butte and is easily visible from the road to Simnasho. All I know about Sidwalter is that it's up in the woods, a long way off the highway, somewhere over near Mount Jefferson. That part of the reservation is closed to non-Indians, and though Dad has a permit that would allow him to take us, he never has. Too busy in the summer. And in the winter, snow chokes off the roads that lead into the woods. I'm excited to get to go as Pinky's guest.

"We turn off up here a ways." Pinky points through the front window down the long, straight stretch of highway.

Pretty soon, Pete slows down and signals with his arm out the window, then downshifts to make the turn. Sidwalter Road is ridged like a washboard and caked in dust. We spew a cloud behind us and shimmy across the road before the tires take hold. The rough, open flat spreads out toward the foothills of the Cascades. The farther we get from the highway, the more the sagebrush and juniper give way to Ponderosa pine and then to deep fir. The rounded, tree-covered knob of HeHe

Butte rises out of the woods to our right, and pretty soon we're in the woods ourselves, leaving the gravel for a winding dirt road. Instantly, the air fills with shadows and the sweet smell of pine.

At first, thick brush presses in on the road from both sides. As we climb, more of the deep blue sky stretches through the trees. The slopes that face north are shadowed thick with timber, and a deep green foliage covers the open and sunny slopes that face south.

"Huckleberries." Pinky points out the window. "They'll be ripe in a few weeks." The air through the window lifts a clean, spicy scent into the cab.

Pete keeps the truck in the middle of the rutted track, even on the curves. He is not expecting to meet any traffic. We must have gone several miles when he suddenly points off to the side of the road up ahead.

"Smoke," he says.

Pete slows the truck as we come around a curve. It's only a campfire, carefully set inside a ring of stones in a small clearing beside the road. *Káthla* stands by her black pickup parked near the fire ring.

So this is where they're hiding. There's no sign of Raymond, but I know he must be close by. I didn't tell my dad about their plans last night when I had the chance. And I won't say anything now.

Jewel pulls open the front flap of a tent tucked back into the trees and peers out.

"Hey," Pinky calls across me out the window. "Hi, Jewel!"

As we pass, Pete waves his arm above the driver's-side window. *Káthla* raises her hand in return, but she doesn't smile.

Finally, the road takes a couple more climbing curves and runs straight across the broad top of the butte. We slide to a stop in a clearing.

The first thing I notice are the gray legs of the lookout tower, anchored on four huge concrete slabs. I can't even see where the legs end until we open the door and step out. And then I have to tilt my head back and back, my eyes following an endless zigzag of metal steps all the way to the top, where the tiny lookout cabin finally appears. I think of all the summer nights when Mrs. Wesley's voice reached out of the radio and into my sleep. And now I'm here. A thrill runs up my backbone.

Mrs. Wesley, small so far up, leans out a window and waves.

"We're staying up there?" I ask Pinky. I hadn't thought about how high it would be.

She laughs. "No—there," and she points over to a little cabin I hadn't noticed under the trees.

Pete unties the tarp, reaches into the pickup bed,

and tosses out our stuff. I take the sack of peaches from him before he can dump it on the ground too. "I gotta get back," he says. "You girls have fun up here."

"They will," says a voice behind us. Mrs. Wesley comes around the side of the pickup. She wears a plaid jacket and jeans, her black hair tied back under a scarf. She reaches out to Pinky and to me, hugs us, then stands clutching our shoulders. She smells of warm woods and rose lotion.

Pete grins, gives her a quick kiss, and gets back in the truck. He is careful not to gun the engine and raise a cloud of dust. The pickup disappears down the curve, but I can hear him changing the gears for a long way before the woods swallow up the sound and he is gone.

"Welcome to Sidwalter," Mrs. Wesley says.

Taller Than the Trees

MRS. Wesley leads us into the cabin and fixes lunch while we store our things in the apple box Pinky uses for a dresser. It takes no time to settle in — the cabin is just one square room. I take in the whole space in four quick turns. Right by the door, a desk and a radio like the one in our hallway, then a bed and some crates beside one window, table and three chairs under another, and a wooden counter and tiny stove at the third. Almost no space left over in the middle. Pinky and I will sleep outside, our bags spread on a tarp under the trees.

As we clean up, I see how much harder it is to live out in the woods than at home. Mrs. Wesley heats a kettle on the stove while Pinky and I haul more water from the big tank outside so that we can wash the dishes. All the food has to go back into the icebox or in a big tin box under the counter to keep it away from mice indoors and bears outside. And because there is so little room in the cabin, everything that is brought out to fix lunch has to be put away. "Or else we'll be tripping over it," Mrs. Wesley tells me as she heads for the tower and back to work.

Pinky and I put everything away. We sweep the whole floor and set the chairs and table straight. A breeze through the open windows cools the cabin.

Then she says, "Wanna go up in the tower?"

I'm not so sure. "It's... tall."

I'm dying to see the view from up there. But the thought of all those stairs and the open weave of steel leaves my knees a little weak.

"Not so bad when it's calm," she says. "C'mon."

When we step out from the shelter of the trees around the cabin, the air is hot. A big space all the way around the lookout has been cleared of trees. "Fire break," Pinky says.

Before starting up the steps, she stops and turns around. "I'll go first. Just keep climbing. *Don't* look down."

I take a deep breath and follow her step by step up

the stairs. She smiles back at me at the first landing, then takes the next set two at a time. By the time I reach the third landing, she has sprinted far ahead.

I am now taller than the trees, and I risk a quick look out across the woods. Mount Jefferson spreads its crisp glacier and rock shoulders before me. I've never seen it so close. The sky is bright and blue, only a whisper of breeze puffs around my arms. So far so good. The wind picks up as I pull myself to the next turn.

Somewhere above me, Pinky crawls through the trapdoor at the top. "Did you leave Kitty down there by herself?" I hear Mrs. Wesley ask.

"Nah—she's coming."

I force my eyes back onto the tower steps and try not to think about how many I still have to climb. Or about the hard ground far below. I grip the railing tight and will myself not to look down.

I finally reach the top, where Pinky holds the trapdoor open for me. I climb through and sag against the table in the center of the tiny space.

"You made it," says Mrs. Wesley, smiling. "Not everyone does." That makes me feel great.

It's definitely worth it. From here, Mount Jefferson feels close enough to touch. And every side opens up a stunning view that I never imagined I'd see all at once and from this high up.

Pinky counts off the peaks in front of us. "Broken Top, Three Fingered Jack. And way down there"—she points off to the southeast—"The Three Sisters." She pulls me around to the other side of the tower and points out the Mutton Mountains, which rise up under a carpet of dry grass and are dotted with dark trees. Then the spindly legs of the fire lookout rising from the bald crest of Eagle Butte.

Like the main cabin below, the tower cabin has no extra space. A big table, the fire finder, takes up the center of the floor. A huge map of the reservation covers the whole surface. We have one in the hall beside the radio at home. Like our map, this one has wavy lines that trace the mountains, hills, and creek drainages. A topographical map, my dad told me when he first put it up. The whole lay of the land spread out on paper. This one has Sidwalter Butte at the center, then lines fanned out to the lookouts on the other buttes—Beaver, Eagle, and Shitike.

In the corner is a bucket with water in it. Rags hang over the side like wicks. "We make sure we have water," Mrs. Wesley says. "That's my first job every morning—bringing it all the way up here."

Pinky pulls a short wooden stool out from under the table, scoots it over to the window, and hops up on it. A small glass cup on each leg—a lightning stool.

I recognize it even though I've never seen one before. Dad said the lookouts stand on them when they use the radio during storms, in case lightning strikes the tower.

My eyes scan the skyline, looking for clouds. Caught up here in a storm—I can't imagine how scary that would be.

Mrs. Wesley stands at the far window holding binoculars to her eyes. Pinky picks up a pair and hands them to me. "Guess how far you can see with these things."

They're heavy, and the view is jiggly until I steady my arms against the windowsill. I get the lenses focused, and all of a sudden I'm staring at the jagged rock face of Eagle Butte, miles and miles across the reservation.

"Gosh—there's the lookout!"

Mrs. Wesley lowers her glasses and glances over her shoulder to see where I'm looking. "Wave to Millie," she says, and laughs.

The radio squawks to life on the shelf beside me. "Afternoon check-in," Mrs. Wesley says. She reaches over and takes the microphone.

One by one, the lookouts report in, bouncing off Mr. Wirt, the dispatcher who sits in the basement of Fire Control at Warm Springs. His voice scratches out of the speaker, followed by each woman's reply. Nothing at Eagle, nothing at Shitike.

Mrs. Wesley tells him that she has a visitor but that all is quiet out in the woods. She signs off, replaces the mike, and then scans the last section of window with the binoculars. After a moment she holds still, twisting the focus slowly with her finger. "Smoke," she says.

Pinky and I both peer out the window in the direction she is looking. Not far off across the woods, but right down below the butte: a thread of whitish smoke. "Oh," says Pinky, "that's just Jewel from our class, with her *káthla*. We passed by their camp on the way up."

Mrs. Wesley shakes her head. "I hope they're careful—it's so dry out here."

⚔️

Later in the afternoon, Pinky and I make our way back down the tower to play cards in the cabin. Climbing down is much worse than going up—no way to fool my eyes about where we are at each step. A couple of moments of panic make me grip the railing to stop my legs from shaking. But I make it down—and maybe I could make it back up again too, I think proudly.

We get through a few games of Hearts, then some Slap Jack and War. Pretty soon, Mrs. Wesley comes in the screen door and says, "Supper time. Girls, go wash up."

Washing up means going around the side of the cabin and pulling a wash pan down from a shelf next to a water barrel. This is on the east side, shaded from the late-afternoon sun.

"Rain," says Pinky, dipping water out of the barrel. "Whatever comes out of the sky and down the roof goes in here. This is for washing and for up in the tower." She points over to two tanks on steel legs resting up against the cabin. "Drinking water has to be hauled from the river. Propane comes from Warm Springs."

Pinky hands me the Ivory bar, and I lather up while she pours a trickle of water. Then I hold my hands out over the basin, and she sloshes a little bit more to rinse. Most of the soap comes off. The rest I wipe with the towel hanging from a nail on the side of the cabin. When I'm done, Pinky hangs the dipper back on the side of the barrel and closes the lid. She splashes her hands through the soapy water in the basin and then dries them. Four hands washed in the water I'd use for two. It must not rain that often up here.

Mrs. Wesley stands at the counter as we walk in. "How about some smoked fish?"

"Yes, please," I say quickly.

She smiles and hands me the plate to put on the table, then pulls a pitcher of water out of the icebox in the corner. Pinky brings a bowl of boiled potatoes, and we sit down. Then Mrs. Wesley pours a small sip of water into the cup set beside each place. I pick up my cup when they do.

"We thank the Creator for giving us this food," she tells me. She and Pinky each take a sip, so I do too. Like saying grace at home.

After supper, Pinky and I wash the dishes. She talks to me about the school year starting up next month, and I'm grateful for her chatter. So much went on during the day that I had no time to think about Jewel and Raymond. In the quiet of the evening, their troubles seep in with the shadows that grow as the light dims. The burden of what I know weighs me down.

At the radio, Mrs. Wesley signs off for the night, "Sidwalter over and out." Then she lays out a tarp under the trees beside the cabin, and we unroll our sleeping bags. I lie there looking up at the black trees outlined by stars. A soft wind crackles through the branches.

Somewhere in the dark down below, I imagine Jewel and Raymond hiding out with *Káthla,* hoping for the best.

Remember the Last Time

IN the morning, when we come back into the cabin after washing the breakfast dishes, Mrs. Wesley hands Pinky a bowl. She lifts up a dishtowel to show us the last of the peaches that Mom sent up. "You girls take these down to Jewel's camp," she says. "They might enjoy some fresh fruit."

The morning is quiet around us, just a rustle of breeze through the leaves. Pinky shows me the path, a shortcut through the brush that disappears down the hill on the far side of the outhouse.

She picks up our conversation about school this year. Pretty soon, we'll be riding the bus up to the junior high in Madras. Changing classes, eating in the cafeteria. No recess, and much more homework. And boys. And maybe lipstick. And a lot we don't even know about.

We reach the road right where it begins to flatten out, and I can smell the campfire. Then I see the corner of the canvas tent around a curve. The camp looks deserted, and the pickup is gone.

"*Hello,*" Pinky calls out. We stand in the road, waiting. Then Pinky takes a few steps forward. "Jewel?"

The brush behind us crackles, and a voice yanks me back almost a whole year to a road not much different from this one. "What do *you* want?"

We whirl to face him. Raymond grips a baseball bat in one hand, his other fist clenched.

Jewel pushes through the brush. "Put that thing down," she tells him, but he shakes his head.

I hold out the bowl — "Mrs. Wesley sent these" — and I lift up the towel to show her. "She thought your grandmother would like them."

Jewel nods her thanks and takes the peaches. We walk with her over to the campfire, where she sets the bowl in the shade of the tent.

"Where's your *káthla*?" Pinky asks.

"She took the truck to check on the berry fields — see when they'll be ripe," Jewel says. She glances at me. "It's just a little ways. She wanted us to stay here."

And she told you to stay out of sight.

Raymond disappears back into the woods, and the three of us sit down at the campfire. Pinky starts in again about all the great things we have to look forward to at the junior high, like dances and football games. She even gets Jewel to smile a little bit.

Suddenly, something makes Jewel hold up her hand. "Wait!" she says with such force that Pinky stops in midsentence. Jewel jumps to her feet, listening.

Then I hear an engine working hard through the gears up the long road grade below. The sound fades in and out with the switchbacks through the woods. "Your *káthla*'s coming back," I say.

Jewel's eyes are wide. Instantly, I know it's not *Káthla* who is speeding up that road. "You have to get out of here," says Jewel. *"Now."*

"What's wrong?" Pinky looks from Jewel to me, frowning.

Walter is coming after Raymond and Jewel. There's no place they can hide and be safe. And there's nothing we can do about it.

Jewel stands frozen, staring off through the brush where the engine grinds louder around the curves below the hill. "Tell me!" Pinky grabs her arm. "What's going on?"

Her voice brings Jewel back into herself. She turns and points up toward the lookout. "Get your mom. We've got big trouble down here."

Pinky's eyes are huge, but she nods. "You guys come too."

Jewel shakes her head. "I can't leave Raymond." I wonder if he's close enough to hear all this.

"C'mon," Pinky says to me, and I'm ready to run with her up the hill, get as far away from here as possible. But Jewel can't face Walter by herself. "I have to stay." My eyes meet Pinky's, and the words tumble out of my mouth. "Tell your mom to call the police. Get Mr. Wewa. Tell him it's Raymond's stepfather, and he'll know what to do."

It must be something in my face that makes Pinky take off running. Or maybe it's the sound of the car almost to the top of the rise.

Jewel grabs my arm and pulls me around the side of the tent as Pinky disappears up the road. The thick brush slashes at us as we scramble through it. We duck under the low branches of a Douglas fir and flop down into the tangle of roots at its base. I peer through the brush, watching the road and trying to quiet my gasping breath.

The car swerves around the curve and lurches to a stop right in front of the tent. Walter sits behind the wheel, staring at the camp. Then he opens the door and gets out, slamming it behind him. "Where is he?" he shouts.

Walter sways a bit, then braces his hand against the car roof to steady himself. *He's been drinking.*

Jewel draws in a sharp breath, and I tuck my shoulder up next to hers. I can feel her tremble.

Walter takes a few steps around the front of the car, keeping his hand on the hood. His boots scuff through the dirt, raising little puffs of dust. He looks around at the camp, at the woods. Like he can see through the brush. "You can't hide from me." Like he knows we're close by.

I'm sure he can't see us, but I have to fight the urge to run.

Walter steps across the ditch at the side of the road, and bats open the tent flap. I hear him inside, ugly sounds of ripping and smashing. When he comes back out, the sunlight glints off the long blade of a knife in his hand. He holds it like he knows how to use it.

I bury my face in the crook of my arm, unable to watch and afraid my pounding heart will give us away.

Walter throws his voice out across the woods. "I got all day."

Heavy, unsteady steps crackle the underbrush. They move away from where we're huddled under the tree. Still, I imagine I can feel the tremor of his steps through the ground.

The woods are silent, as if the birds and the wind

have also gone into hiding. All I can hear is Walter thrashing through the bushes. Away from us for a few minutes, and then back. Then I get it — Walter is searching in a deliberate zigzag, first one direction, and then the other. The stuff he smashed in the tent, the bowl of peaches, the embers still warm in the fire ring. He *knows* Jewel and Raymond are here.

Please, God, help us.

Jewel gasps, a sudden, tiny breath beside me. He's coming. In a few seconds, he's going to see us.

"Don't move," Jewel whispers so low I can barely hear her. And then, amazingly, she pushes herself up off the ground and scrambles away from the tree.

She's trying to protect me.

The footsteps stop. "You thought you could get away from me." Walter taunts her, low and mean.

I've never heard a grownup talk like this.

There's nothing to stop him from hurting her. But maybe he won't in front of me. And I'm too scared to stay here by myself. I take a deep breath and get up too. Walter's eyes narrow when he sees me. I brush at the dirt clinging to my knees and elbows, then go stand beside Jewel.

Walter towers over us. Close enough that I can see the crinkled lines on his face, the puffy redness of his eyes. Catch a whiff of the sweet sickness on his breath.

"The old lady can keep the little creep," he says to Jewel. "But you're going with me."

Walter reaches to grab hold of Jewel's wrist, but she twists away. She yanks me by the arm, and we make a dash for the road. We jump to the other side of the fire pit as Walter lumbers around the side of the tent.

He stops short, breathing hard, and stares at us across the smoldering coals. Sweat has popped out across his forehead, but his eyes are ice cold. "Oh, you *are* going with me."

He holds up the knife and points the blade at Jewel.

"No!" Jewel pants, wilting like all the fight has gone out of her.

I'm terrified, but I've got to do *something*. I bend and pull a piece of kindling out of the fire. I hand the cool end to Jewel and then pick up another one.

Jewel holds the glowing stick out in front of her. "What do you think you're going to do with *that?*" Walter smirks. Jewel is shaking now. We hold each other up.

He steps slowly around the edge of the campfire. I grab Jewel's arm, and we move when he does, keeping the burning ends of the kindling pointed at his chest. We've got to stay out of reach of that knife.

A sudden movement catches my eye, and I'm startled by an explosion of shattering glass. *The car.*

"What the hell!" Walter roars.

I spin around in time to see Raymond swing the bat high over his shoulder and blast out the second headlight. Then he grips the bat with both hands, holds it across his chest like a rifle. "Get out!" he screams. His voice is like a steel door slamming shut.

Walter looks wild with rage. He holds up the knife and takes a step toward Raymond. "Remember the last time." He spits out the words.

Raymond nods slowly. His eyes never leave Walter's face. "That will *never* happen again." He lifts the bat and destroys the window on the passenger side.

Walter jerks back like he'd been struck.

Jewel grabs my arm, and I see fire in her eyes again. "You're a coward!" she shouts. "Beating up on kids and old ladies." I hear fear and pain in her voice — and courage, too.

The first shadow of uncertainty flickers across Walter's face. He slowly moves toward his battered car, keeping a wary eye on Raymond. He opens the door and rests his boot on the running board. "You're worthless trash," he says. "Both of you." He gets behind the wheel. Before he can turn the key, I hear a second engine roaring up the road.

A tribal police car rounds the curve, red light pulsing on the roof. It skids sideways, blocking the road.

Mr. Wewa jumps out of the cruiser, runs to Walter's car, and pulls him from the driver's seat.

In an instant, Walter's arms are shackled behind his back. He struggles to stand upright. "Get your dirty hands off me!" he yells.

Mr. Wewa stands in front of him, his hand resting on the holster at his hip. "Sir, you are under arrest."

"I didn't do nothing!"

Mr. Wewa holds up the knife. "Aggravated assault," he says, "and trespassing on tribal land."

Walter sneers. "You can't touch me."

"Well, I'm afraid you're wrong about that," Mr. Wewa says calmly. "Those are federal offenses. You can take it up with the FBI."

As Mrs. Wesley and Pinky come running down the hill, Mr. Wewa leads Walter to the cruiser, eases him down into the back seat, and slams the door. He takes a quick look at the broken windows and the shards of glass around Walter's car. "You kids OK?" he asks.

Still gripping the bat, Raymond nods.

Mr. Wewa studies Raymond, his face serious. "That was a dangerous thing to do," he says. Then his eyes soften. "But it was also very brave."

Raymond's expression doesn't change. I wonder if he has ever heard something like that from a grownup before.

Beside me, Jewel's shoulders begin to shake. She hasn't said a thing since Mr. Wewa arrived. Now she puts her hands up to her face and sobs.

Mrs. Wesley touches Jewel's shoulder. "It's OK, sweetie," she says. "It's over now."

Jewel looks at Mr. Wewa through her tears. "You stopped him," she says, disbelief in her voice.

"We would have tried a long time ago," he says gently. "If someone had told us how he was treating you. You have your friend to thank for that."

Mr. Wewa turns to me. "When the call came in, I was already on the road. Following a hunch about places where people might want to hide."

Mr. Wewa did *listen, and he believed me.* Gratitude floods my heart.

⋘⊰HOH⊱⋙

Mrs. Wesley gathers us together and takes us back to the lookout. Jewel pins a note to the tent for her grandmother. On the hike up the hill, Pinky tells how she ran up the shortcut, then took the tower stairs two at a time. Once she could catch her breath and talk, Mrs. Wesley spread the word on the radio, and both Mr. Wewa and my dad responded.

"I told your dad what was happening," Mrs. Wesley says. "He'll come pick you up if you want to go home."

My heart is still beating hard, but I feel safe now

that Walter is gone. And I'd hate to miss this time with my friends. "No—I want to stay."

She smiles and nods. Then she puts all of us to work fixing lunch.

Káthla drives up as we start to eat. When she steps down from the pickup, her face is creased with worry, but she smiles when she sees Jewel and Raymond. She hugs them hard. Mrs. Wesley pulls out another plate, and we kids take ours out under the trees so that *Káthla* can sit at the table.

Raymond sits on a log off by himself, hunched over his food. I can't read his face. He hasn't said anything since Mr. Wewa locked Walter in the police car. I can't believe that someone would really pull a knife and say those things. I'm still shaky.

Pinky takes a bite of sandwich. "This might finally do it," she says.

"Do what?" asks Jewel.

"Get him out of your life."

Jewel stops chewing. Her shoulders suddenly relax. "Maybe," she says softly.

For the first time, I hear hope in her voice.

A Different Kind of Thunder

MRS. Wesley invites *Káthla* to move the camp up to the clearing by the tower, but she shakes her head. "We're fine now. We can go home in the morning."

Raymond and Jewel climb into the pickup, we say goodbye, and *Káthla* steers her old truck back down the hill. I watch until they are out of sight around the curve, the rumble of the engine swallowed by the trees.

That evening, Pinky and I sweep up the cabin after supper. At the radio, Mrs. Wesley signs off for the night.

"One last thing," says Mr. Wirt through the speaker. "Weather service says there's a front comin' in. Keep an eye on your weather station. Over."

"Ten-four," Mrs. Wesley says. "Sidwalter over and out." She twists the volume down but leaves the power on.

"A storm?" I ask. I think of all the fires started by lightning this summer.

Mrs. Wesley puts her hand on my arm and smiles. "I'm headed out to check. Come see."

The three of us walk out into the evening — it's so much cooler up here than at home. Almost jacket weather. I scan for clouds across the fading sky.

At the edge of the cleared area under the tower stands a small wooden box on metal legs, kind of like a square white beehive on stilts. When we get closer, I see that it's made of wooden slats like shutters. Mrs. Wesley lifts a latch and pulls the side down toward her. Inside is a simple box with what looks like Bill's science kit — a glass tube, a battery, a thermometer.

She leans in to check the tube. "He could be right," she says. "Barometer's down from this morning. Change coming." Then she looks at my face. "But you don't need to worry." *Just like my mom.*

All of a sudden, everything from this long day sweeps over me, and my heart starts hammering again. I shut my eyes and try to breathe in and out slowly.

"Oh, honey," Mrs. Wesley says gently. She lays a hand on my shoulder. Her touch is warm. She pulls Pinky close with her other arm. "You've both been through a lot today."

"I was so scared," I finally say. "I didn't want to be, but I couldn't help it."

"Me either," says Pinky.

"But you went for help," I say.

Mrs. Wesley smiles. "And you stayed. You kids all looked out for each other." Mrs. Wesley gestures toward the road that winds down away from the tower. "Let's take a walk and enjoy the evening." Pinky and I fall into step with her. The breeze is quiet, moving with us through the gathering dark.

"A long time ago," Mrs. Wesley says after a bit, "the Creator placed the people where we needed to be so that we could care for everything around us. We are Wasco — the Creator placed us on the Big River, Nch'i-wána."

"The Columbia," I say. Mrs. Wesley nods.

As the road winds down the hill, the trees and brush hold the cool air close to us. Overhead, the light fades from the sky, and a few stars blink through.

"I was born near Celilo Falls," she continues, "where the river thundered over the rocks before the dams were built."

In the museum at the back of McKenzie's store, I've seen photos of the men fishing with long poles and nets. They stood on wooden platforms that stuck out over the river but were anchored to the rocks. The water rumbled under their feet. A skinny rope tied around the fisherman's waist was his only safety harness. It must have been scary, but Indian people had fished at Celilo forever.

"Even though we now live at Warm Springs," Mrs. Wesley says, "we've never left the river."

The road is now almost completely shadowed. We walk a little bit farther, to the turnoff that disappears down the far side of the hill and ends up at Jewel's camp.

"I wish I was from somewhere powerful like that," I say quietly.

Mrs. Wesley smiles. "The Creator has also placed you where you need to be." Then she turns, and we make our way back up the hill. I wonder what she means exactly.

I feel better at bedtime, but I don't want to sleep outside. Instead, Mrs. Wesley lays out my sleeping bag on the floor right in front of the door, the only open spot in the cabin. Pinky curls up on the bed with her mom. We say good night, and Mrs. Wesley turns out the propane light.

My sleeping bag is a soft cocoon, even on the hard floor. The red light on the battery-powered radio blinks above my head. The faint hiss of static sounds like water. As I drift toward sleep, I listen for Celilo Falls tumbling over boulders far away.

⋘⊰HO⊱⋙

I'm thrust awake in what feels like an instant. Bright light flashes at the window.

I scrunch down in the bag, flatten my hands over my ears, and count. *One, one thousand. Two, one thousand.* In seconds, thunder kabooms over the cabin and rumbles off over the crest of the hill.

A second searing bolt flashes through the sleeping bag and my closed eyelids, followed instantly by an explosion that rocks the cabin. I curl up into a ball, as far down in the bag as I can get.

Above me, the bedsprings creak. Mrs. Wesley must be pulling on her jeans, scooting her boots out from under the bed. The wind sprays dust and pine needles against the window.

"Mom?" Pinky's sleepy voice.

"Just a bad storm," Mrs. Wesley says. "I gotta go up." The lightning shreds the dark, and thunder comes in waves. She's going up in the tower in *this?*

Mrs. Wesley is out of the cabin in seconds. As she steps over me, I feel her lean down and put her hand on my bag. She touches the top of my head. "It's OK

· 213 ·

to be scared," she says firmly. And then she bangs out the door.

I hear Pinky get out of bed and strike a match under the propane lamp by the wall. In a moment, static erupts into the cabin. Pinky has turned up the radio. She stands by the desk, her foot bumping into my backside.

Soon I hear Mrs. Wesley sign on, her voice punctuated by screeching static. Each lightning strike chops through the transmission with a shriek.

"Station One, this is Sidwalter. Come in," she says.

Her voice is even, no different from the hundred times I've heard it at home. But I'm startled to recognize the voice that responds from the hallway outside my bedroom in Warm Springs. Clear and deep and strong. "This is Station One. Go ahead, Sidwalter." My dad, awake and ready.

"Station One. We've got a storm right on top of us. Over," Mrs. Wesley says.

"Roger, Sidwalter," my dad replies. "Keep your eye on it." The radio hums and pulses with the lightning. Thunder batters us from above.

Suddenly, Mrs. Suppah breaks in from Eagle Butte. I can barely recognize her voice. She must be shouting into the microphone. *"Sidwalter, come in!"*

Mrs. Wesley responds, "Go ahead, Eagle."

"First—Station One, you've gotta get a crew to Sidwalter *right now*," Mrs. Suppah says. "And Sidwalter..." She takes a breath, then says strongly, "You need to get those kids up top!"

"Come again, Eagle?" Mrs. Wesley asks. I hear the first hint of worry in her voice. A flash of lightning, another instant crack of thunder, and the radio goes dead.

I pull my head out of the sleeping bag and just make out Pinky's silhouette at the window. *"Oh my God,"* she says, choking.

Underneath the storm's fury I hear a different kind of thunder, out of sight below the hill. Like the roar of a freight train coming up fast.

I throw off the sleeping bag and lurch to the window. Before my eyes can adjust to the dark, Pinky pushes past me. "Come on!" she yells. I turn and see her now at the door, pulling on her shoes, hopping on one foot.

Come on – where? More thunder crashes down on our heads. I want to crawl back into my sleeping bag, but Pinky grips my arm and pushes my shoes into my hands. "Put these on!" Automatically, I do as she says.

She flings open the door. I can't believe she wants me to go out there! She grabs my hand and drags me into the wind and around the side of the cabin, both of us still in our pajamas. She plucks two towels off the nails above the wash basin and dunks them quickly into the rain barrel.

"Here!" she shouts, thrusting a dripping towel into my hands. "You're gonna need this."

The noise in my head blots out everything else. I can't begin to grasp what's coming next. The roar grows around the sides of the cabin. When we step out into the open, I feel heat for the first time. Pinky is pulling me toward the base of the tower when it finally registers.

Fire.

I stop and look back down the road. Along both sides, flames now ravage the underbrush. Sparks leap high into the air, swallowing the road where we walked earlier this evening.

The only way out.

Into the Burning Night

I'VE never heard anything so loud. I stand stunned, unable to move. Pinky reaches back and yanks hard on my arm. "Kitty!" she shouts. "We gotta *go!*"

She pulls me over the ground. She is strong for such a scrawny kid. I focus on the tower steps before us. This time, I leap for them as she does, taking two at a time.

We sprint upward as the smoke chases us and snags around our heads. Pinky holds a wet towel up to her face and signals to me to do the same. I wrap the towel around my nose and mouth, stumbling behind her.

We scramble toward the top, faster and faster. No time to catch our breath at the landings. The smoke rises faster than we can climb, but we battle upward through it. Pinky trips and goes down hard on a step, the metal grating biting into her knee. I help her up, and we keep going. Blood drips onto each step as we pass.

I don't have time to be afraid. We just climb as fast as we can through the suffocating fog. We keep going, breathing hard, not talking. Thunder booms down on us, lightning photographs the mountains around us.

I've lost track of how far we've gone. When I reach up for the next railing, my hand meets strong arms. Mrs. Wesley bends down to pull me up to the last landing. She reaches out, grasps Pinky under her arms, and hefts her up onto her hip. Mrs. Wesley reaches back and clasps me around the wrist. I don't know how she does it, but she hauls us to safety and bangs the trapdoor shut.

Mrs. Wesley yanks the wet towels from our faces and tucks them quickly into the cracks around the trap door. Sealing out the smoke. Then she points to the wooden bucket under the fire table, where I find new cloths, already wet. "Tie a mask around your nose and mouth!" she yells.

I hold the cloth to my face while Mrs. Wesley tends to Pinky. She is a mess — her leg bleeding furiously now and her face pale.

"Is she OK?" My voice is muffled through the towel.

Mrs. Wesley nods quickly, wrapping a wet towel

around Pinky's leg. Pinky starts to cry, holding tight to her mother's arm.

Mrs. Wesley speaks to her quickly, softly. "I need you to be strong now. You gotta stay focused. Sit here while I call in." I hear the worry in her voice.

I sit with Pinky on the wood floor, in the corner of the tower. I tie the mask securely to my face, and I help Pinky tie hers, too. I put my arm around her as she holds the towel to her knee.

Mrs. Wesley stands up and reaches for the radio next to the fire table. She clicks the microphone. "Station One — Sidwalter... Station One — Sidwalter... Come in, Station One," she repeats.

This time there is no static.

"We can't raise them," she says quietly as her hands scramble over the radio, checking wires, pushing buttons. Trying to get it to work. *"Come on,"* she says.

Suddenly, we catch the tail end of Dad's transmission. "...you there?" *Oh, I wish I'd let him come for me yesterday.*

"Station One — trouble with the radio," Mrs. Wesley responds, and it goes out again.

I hear something underneath the storm — the frenzied honking of a horn. Mrs. Wesley looks down through the window, her face reflected in the strange orange glow.

"Oh, no," she says. "They didn't get out!"

I'm scared to look, but I go to the window. *Káthla*'s truck hurtles up the road, right through the tunnel of flames, and skids to a stop at the cabin. My whole body starts to shake as Raymond jumps out from behind the wheel and pounds on the cabin door. Jewel helps her grandmother out of the pickup. *Káthla* leans heavily on her.

Mrs. Wesley turns to me. "Kitty," she says, "you've got to go down and help them get up here."

My heart catches. *"Me?"*

She takes both of my shoulders in her hands and leans down to face me head-on. "I have to stay here, get the radio to work so they know what's going on."

My shoulders shake under her hands. I know Pinky can't be the one to go. But I'm not sure I can, either. Mrs. Wesley holds me firmly, looks right in my eyes. "You have to help them. And you have to do it right now."

She grabs two more wet cloths, ties one around my nose and mouth and the other over my head. She thrusts the bucket into my hands. "Take all of these. Make them cover up. Then get them up here as fast as you can."

Mrs. Wesley scrapes the towels from around the trap door and lifts it. "You can do this," she says firmly.

Smoke boils into the tower. I'm shaking so hard, I can barely grip the bucket handle, but I take a deep breath, clamp my mouth shut, and start the long climb down. Above me, the trapdoor bangs shut. I hear Mrs. Wesley slide open a window. She leans out, yelling, *"Up here! Up here!"*

Smoke and sparks swirl around the tower steps, and I can't see anything down below.

I cling to the railing with one hand, feel for each stair with my foot. Concentrate on one step at a time, counting the turns I remember from yesterday. Six steps down to a landing, turn, six steps to the next landing. Take short breaths. Ignore the heat that blasts in my face. Don't drop the bucket. Don't think about anything else.

I don't see any more lightning, and the thunder has moved off to the east. What's left is the howl of the fire.

Through the smoke, I finally hear a voice not far below me. "One more, *Káthla.* That's it." Strong, no hint of urgency. *Raymond?* "Now another. Keep going."

Then Jewel. "It's OK. Hang on to me."

I can't see them, but I grip the bucket tighter, slide my hand more quickly down the railing, and call out, *"Jewel!* Keep coming up!"

I find the next landing and hang there, breathing hard. The smoke is so thick, I feel it seep into my lungs even through the mask. It's all I can do to keep my balance.

A hand reaches up and seizes my wrist. Raymond pulls himself and his *káthla* up to the landing. I reach out to grasp her arm and help him ease her down onto a step.

I grab wet cloths out of the bucket and thrust them at Raymond. "Quick! Tie this around *Káthla*'s face!" I order. "And these are for you and Jewel!"

He carefully covers his grandmother's face. Jewel coughs as she pulls herself up to the landing, breathing hard, and hugs her grandmother.

"Jewel!" I say sharply. "You've got to get this on your face!"

She just slumps down at *Káthla*'s side.

The flames below have grown, and the roar builds and spreads up toward us. It's oven hot here on this landing, and the sparks and embers fly around our heads.

I tug on Jewel's arm. *"Move!"* I scream.

Raymond looks at me, lifts his grandmother off the landing, and starts to carry her up the stairs. I grab Jewel's sleeve, and she reacts with the strength I know she has in her. Together, we stumble up the long steps, grasping the rails one after another.

Smoke and sparks lick at our feet. We work our way upward, pulling each other, until at last we reach the open trapdoor. Mrs. Wesley has helped Raymond boost his grandmother inside. Jewel and I scramble up until we're on the solid floor of the tower and Mrs. Wesley can slam the door shut against the fire.

Mrs. Wesley helps *Káthla* settle down onto the floor. Raymond and Jewel gather her between them. I stuff the towels back into the cracks around the trapdoor, then sneak a peek at the window to catch the pulsing reflection of fire in the trees below.

Mrs. Wesley sits down and lifts Pinky into her lap. Pinky hunkers down in her mother's arms. I go sit against the wall beside them, and Mrs. Wesley curls her arm tight around my shoulders. "It's going to be OK," she says. She rubs her palm around the top of my arm. "They will get help to us."

Smoke seeps into the tower, even through the towels stuffed around the door. I can feel the heat through the floorboards and see sparks flying past the window. *How did they get so high?*

I can't help it now — my whole body shakes hard, even under Mrs. Wesley's soothing hand. Pinky must be feeling the fear too. Buried in her mother's arms, she lets out little whimpers. But there's no shame in being afraid. Without Pinky, I would never have been able to get up into the tower or help Jewel and Raymond and *Káthla*.

"It will get warm in here," Mrs. Wesley says through the cloth. "The smoke will rise up, and some of it will get in. But we'll have enough air to breathe. This tower's mostly metal. It's not going to burn. We just need to stay put."

I know she's trying to keep us calm. She can't possibly know that we'll be OK. But I want to believe her. "There's nothing we can do?" I ask. I'm afraid to say the words out loud, but I have to know.

Mrs. Wesley tightens her arm around me. "We did what we had to by getting up here. Now we're going to hold on." Her voice is soothing, and I relax a little.

A hot wind buffets the tower, sniffing the walls like a wolf after a rabbit. The roar from below grows as the smoke puffs more quickly through the cracks. Mrs. Wesley lets go of my shoulder for a moment and takes the mask from Pinky's mouth. She reaches over to the bucket, dips the cloth to wet it again, and hands it back. Then she does the same for *Káthla,* for me, for Jewel, and for Raymond and then finally for herself.

Mrs. Wesley's hand is now moist on my arm. I try to match my breathing to hers, but I can't hold still the great shaking that has taken me over.

Quietly, *Káthla* begins to sing, a tune that softly rises and falls, with words I don't understand. In a moment, Mrs. Wesley lifts her head and hums. Jewel, Raymond, and Pinky join in.

I lean back against the wall and close my eyes. As the heat builds in the tiny room, we send our prayers out into the burning night.

The Charred Duff

I lift my head to the gray light that filters into the tower. Right away, I know that my bottom hurts. And when I move my head, my neck is stiff and sore. I sit up, and Mrs. Wesley stirs beside me. Her arm still rests on my shoulder, though now there is no grip in her hand, only weight.

It takes a moment for me to realize that the smoke is gone. We are still here, breathing in the cool, dark air. All of us are huddled in the corner of the tower, backs against the raw wooden slats of the walls. *Káthla* seems to be holding up Raymond and Jewel. Pinky's head lolls far over her mother's arm. Mrs. Wesley must be numb, I think.

She shakes herself awake. "You OK?" she asks.

I nod my head, not yet ready to speak. When I look up at the window above our heads, I can see stars.

Mrs. Wesley leans over and kisses the top of my head. "We made it," she says.

She gently touches Pinky's face, waking her. Slowly, we shift onto our knees. Carefully testing our bodies.

Káthla opens her eyes and wraps her arm more firmly around Jewel. Raymond stirs.

I make it to my knees before the pins and needles stab every movement. I rest for a moment, then pull myself up to the window for my first glimpse of the new world below.

"Oh" is all I can say. The fire has taken everything.

Waning moonlight now floods the knob of Sidwalter Butte. There is no forest left here. Only a parade of sentry pines, black and scarred and limbless but still standing. No undergrowth, no small plants: an endless charred carpet.

Mrs. Wesley pulls herself up beside me and stares. Pinky quickly goes from window to window.

"Mom!" she calls. "Come here!"

I peer over her shoulder and see that the cabin still stands. *Káthla's* pickup, untouched, nuzzles up to the porch. Some invisible hand channeled the fire away from the cabin, leaving it untouched in a ring of devastation.

"Well, look at that," says Mrs. Wesley. She gives each of us a big hug and wipes her eyes with the hem of her shirt.

Now I hear honking again — it's rising from somewhere below. Mrs. Wesley opens the window that looks down on the road. An army of pickups and pumpers speeds through the ash and dust and skids to a stop at the top of the rise.

They have come for us!

A wiry man in a red hard hat jumps out of the first pickup. Even before we can shout, he scrambles to the cabin and flings open the door.

Pinky lets loose from up above, screaming, "Dad! We're here! Up here!"

He stops, turns, and runs to the steps as Mrs. Wesley throws open the trapdoor. Pinky scrambles down the stairs as fast as she can, with Mrs. Wesley and me right behind her.

He meets us somewhere in the middle of the tower. Pinky flings herself into his arms, and he has to steady himself on the landing to catch her. Mrs. Wesley joins them, and then he reaches out his arms and gathers me in too. I remember that I'm in my pajamas, but I don't even care.

By now, there is a mob on the tower steps. The

firefighters' faces are grim and gritty. They have been working hard all night, but this is what they've been working for.

Two of them scramble up into the tower cabin. They tenderly carry *Káthla* down the long series of steps. Raymond and Jewel follow close behind.

From up on the tower steps, I see a last pickup lurch to a stop at the top of the road. It is the green we look for every time we drive home during fire season — with the Interior Department buffalo stamped in the paint under the driver's window. That door is flung open, and those familiar boots step into the charred duff.

"Daddy!" I scream from the last landing.

He looks up, and it must be relief flooding into his face, but I can't see clearly now, as I scramble down the rest of the way, past the crew gathering at the bottom, and fold myself into his outstretched arms.

"Oh, baby," he says. Dad holds me so close, all I can smell is sweat and smoke and the fear of this long night in his skin. "Oh, baby," he says again.

<hr>

Káthla rests on the porch of the cabin, wrapped in a blanket, Raymond beside her with his arm around her small shoulders. Mr. Wesley has brought a pitcher and a stack of cups outside. He holds them on a tray while Pinky's mother pours water for the firefighters.

Pinky pushes out through the screen door. She has put on her jeans and a sweatshirt. And then Jewel comes out too, one of Mrs. Wesley's wool jackets over her sooty clothes.

Dad clasps my hand and walks over to the porch. He reaches his other hand out to *Káthla*. She takes it and nods at me. "You be proud of her."

Dad's voice catches. "I am." He wraps his arm around my shoulders and says to Pinky, Jewel, and Raymond, "I'm so proud of all of you."

Raymond lifts his head and meets my dad's eye. Then he nods.

Mrs. Wesley helps me roll up my sleeping bag, and I quickly get dressed and stuff the rest of my clothes back in the knapsack. I can't let myself look out of the window or think about what happened. I just want to go home.

When we come out of the cabin, Dad is shutting the pickup door for *Káthla*. Her truck starts rough, but it runs. Raymond sits beside her on the front seat, Jewel by the window. When they pull out and we lift our hands, Jewel waves back.

The firefighters have fanned out across the knob of

Sidwalter Butte to mop up hot spots. Pinky and her parents will leave as soon as the last spark has cooled.

Dad tucks my things into the back of his pickup. He doesn't mention the government and kids not being allowed to ride in trucks. He just holds open the passenger door for me, and I climb in.

It's a long ride out of the woods. I keep my head down so I don't have to see what the fire took away. Nothing can keep out the sharp sting of smoke that hangs in the air, even with all the windows rolled up. And finally, I give in and let loose the great weight that's been in my heart for what feels like forever. When he's not shifting gears on the bumpy road, Dad keeps his big hand over mine on the seat and lets me cry.

At the highway, Dad waits for a break in a long line of cars coming from Portland. Then he pulls into the lane and points the pickup toward home.

◄◄◄⫴⊙⊩►►►

Mom, Bill, and Joe are all standing out in the yard when we pull into the driveway. Dad radioed ahead to tell them I was safe. It feels so strange to see the worry and relief that flood their faces. For me.

Mom opens the pickup door and wraps me in a hug. "What an ordeal," she says. She keeps her arm around me as we walk toward the house.

Dad tosses the sleeping bag to Joe and carries my knapsack himself. Only when we get out in the open do I smell the smoke that clings to my clothes, to everything that comes out of the truck.

Bill stands on the back steps, holding the screen door open. He bumps his fist gently against my shoulder. "I hear you did good."

It's the best thing he could have said.

It's Our Way

A week after the fire, everything has settled back to normal. One evening, Dad walks in the back door from work as Mom is putting the hamburgers on the table. He pauses in the kitchen doorway. I see him catch Mom's eye and nod. A quick smile passes between them. *What's that about?*

"Big game tonight," Bill says as we sit down.

"You bet," Dad says, forking a burger from the plate and slapping it into a bun.

We're playing Metolius again, at home. Last game of the season.

⫷⫷⫷◁►⫸⫸⫸

When we pull up to the field, Dad parks near the back of the stands. Bill and Joe pile out to join their team.

Mom and Dad greet the other parents and find places in the bleachers.

The boys took off without the big jug of Kool-Aid for the team. I reach into the back of the station wagon to jerk it free.

"I'll take that," says an eager voice behind me.

It's Howie. Same old silly grin on his face and buttoned-up shirt, even in the warm evening. I'm surprised how glad I am to see him.

"Thanks. Can you take it over to Joe?"

"Yup." Howie nods. "My friend Joe."

He carries the jug in both arms over to the bench and sets it in the grass at the edge of the field. Then Howie sits himself down next to Joe. He's not even on the team, but there he is, keeping Joe company on the bench.

I have to smile. *Some people just make everything a little bit better.*

A familiar tribal police car stops next to our station wagon. Mr. Wewa grabs his patrolman's hat and puts it on as he gets out. He sees me and smiles. *What's he doing here?*

Káthla parks her black pickup next to the cruiser. Jewel slides out behind her and helps her grandmother up to the first row of the bleachers. Raymond steps out of the truck with his glove. He hangs back, like he's not sure he belongs here.

Mr. Wewa walks over to him. Raymond looks nervous, turning his glove in his hands.

"Your dad passed away a long time ago," Mr. Wewa says. "You might not know what you're supposed to do to make this right. It's our way."

I expect Raymond to shrug or scowl or act like Mr. Wewa isn't standing there. But he simply shakes his head. "No, sir."

Mr. Wewa leans in and tells him something. Then he steps back. "Son, you let me know what you decide." And he returns to his patrol car and leans up against it, watching the field.

Raymond stands still, like he's trying to make up his mind. Then he takes a deep breath and walks over to Mr. Wewa. "OK," he says. "I'm ready."

Mr. Wewa gives him a nod, and they walk together around the backstop and onto the field. I hurry up into the stands to sit with Mom and Dad, wondering what Raymond's going to do.

Bill is warming up on the mound, throwing strikes to Jimmy, who's behind the plate. He looks up to throw one more, then holds still when he sees Raymond with Mr. Wewa. He signals to Jimmy, then walks off the mound. He goes over to Raymond, puts the ball in Raymond's glove, and calmly heads over to third base.

The players gather around Raymond. They look wary, and so does he. He talks to them for a few minutes, then cocks his head toward the bleachers. The whole team walks over, and everyone gets quiet.

Raymond steps out in front of the team. He pauses for a moment, then speaks loud enough for everyone in the bleachers to hear.

"I'm sorry for hitting the batter," he says. "I threw the ball at his ankle, but I had no argument with him. I know I dishonored my team and Warm Springs. I hope you all will accept my apology."

I look over at my dad beside me. He sits there nodding. Mom, on his other side, reaches for his hand. "Is that what Mr. Wewa worked out—an apology?" I ask.

"Yep." Dad smiles down at me. "It's a custom here," he says. "A good one. You face up to the truth. Take responsibility for the things you do that hurt people. It doesn't change what happened, but you do what you can to make it right."

That took a lot of courage.

Jewel turns to catch my eye. She gives me a warm smile.

Raymond stands in front of the silent bleachers for a few seconds. He looks up into the faces before him, but nobody speaks. After a few moments, he turns and walks away, but he doesn't go to the mound. He walks straight over to the Metolius bench. He stops in front of the kid leaning on crutches at the far end and says something. The red-haired kid nods once, then turns away.

Raymond turns and walks back, tosses the ball to Bill, and sits himself down at the far end of the bench next to Howie.

The umpire steps up to the plate. He points at Bill and calls, "Play ball!" My brother walks to the mound, and the teams take the field and play.

Something to Hold

BILL pitches a shutout. The only threat comes on a fly ball hit straight to Joe in left field. And he catches it. Howie goes nuts with his whooping and clapping.

Warm Springs wraps up the season with a win.

Sherf invites the whole team across the road to his house for pop and ice cream. "C'mon, son"—he points to Howie—"you too."

"We've got some cake at home," Mom says to Dad and me. "We can celebrate too."

I'm surprised when Dad tells her, "Why don't you take the car. Kitty and I can walk. It's a nice evening."

Mom pulls out of the parking lot, then turns at the corner and heads up the road toward McKenzie's. Dad and I take the path that leads past Fire Control, across the bridge over Shitike Creek, and up the hill behind the jail.

He must want to talk to me about something. Maybe the fire. Neither of them has said anything since I got home, like they're waiting for me to bring it up.

Mrs. Wesley went back to the lookout a few days later, but it made her so sad to be up there that she asked to be relieved. Dad sent one of the forestry trainees to finish out the season.

I don't want to think about it anymore.

The last glow of sunset lights up the sky, and the breeze that follows us away from the ball field brings a tinge of fall. School starts in about a month. As we begin to climb the hill, I'm glad I have that to look forward to.

Then Dad stops walking. "Honey, I need to tell you something." He looks down at me. "I got a call from Washington yesterday."

My heart drops. I want to stop the rest of the words from coming.

"Washington, D.C.," I say, turning away.

"Yes. They want me to come work for the commissioner of Indian Affairs."

The nod and the smile when he came home from work.

I focus my eyes on the dark shapes of the rimrock hills beyond the canyon of the Deschutes River, where the highway winds up to the flat plains full of mint. To the east, the direction we'll be going.

"We haven't even been here a whole year." My voice feels tight, and I have to push the words out of my mouth.

"I know, honey," he says. "I'm sorry. But it's an opportunity I can't pass up."

"When?"

Dad sighs. This can't be easy for him, but I don't care.

"I have to start on the first of August. So we leave for Virginia on Tuesday."

Five days.

The light from this baseball sun fades across the sky. Out on the highway, a log truck rumbles as the driver downshifts to ease his load through the long grade from the woods. Then the truck and two cars pass the turnoff to Warm Springs.

I watch them speed by and wonder what lies ahead for me.

⋘✦⋙

The last days in Warm Springs go in a blur of sorting and packing. Mom pulls out the moving boxes we emptied last August, their labels still clear in her neat printing: K'S ROOM, SEWING, KITCHEN. Bill and Joe throw their stuff together, then pack up Dad's workbench as he wraps up the last details at work. They all seem happy and excited.

I move through each day thinking about everything I'm losing. Like my birthday and a party with my friends. Pinky and Jewel would be there, and we'd be making plans for next year. Instead I'll be opening gifts in some motel in Ohio. And when we get to Virginia, I'll have to start all over.

I know that Tuesday will come, and we will lock the back door for the last time, walk down the sidewalk past the zinnias, and get into the station wagon with the tarp roped tight over the bulging cargo rack. We'll pull out of the driveway and leave all this behind forever. The way we always do.

Pinky comes by to say goodbye. She brings me a beaded bracelet and some dried salmon from her mom. And her steelie, the shooter that won her fame in the marbles ring at school. I give her the blond Barbie and the packet of shoes she loves. Pinky starts to tell me about the muffins she'll enter in the Jefferson County fair next week, but she stops when she sees my face. I'll be back in Virginia by then.

Pinky hugs me hard, though she only comes up to my chin. "I'll see you," she says. Then she heads back down the alley toward home. I nod and wave, even though I don't think she ever will.

Tuesday morning, the house is nearly empty. All the dishes are packed, and Mom sends me over to McKenzie's for paper plates so she can fix breakfast. "Just the small pack," she says, handing me money.

The store is crowded with shoppers. As I make my way through the aisles, people stop me to say goodbye. First our neighbor, Mrs. Litton. Then Mrs. Wyatt from the school office. Finally, Mr. McKenzie himself.

When I push through the glass doors, Jewel and *Káthla* are standing beside their truck. "We went by your house," Jewel says. "Your mom said you were over here."

I nod, holding up the paper sack. "All our plates are packed."

Jewel suddenly looks shy. "We're going up to see my cousin. Do you want to come?"

It takes me a moment to understand what she means. The cemetery.

"Your mother said to tell you she can wait," *Káthla* says, nodding toward the sack.

"OK, then — sure."

Káthla opens the pickup door, and I follow Jewel around to the passenger side. Then I stop.

"I need something," I say, tilting my head toward the store. "I'll be right back."

The cemetery spreads across the top of a bald knob way out on the reservation. *Káthla* turns in at a gate and then drives slowly over the bare track lined with wild-flowers and cheatgrass. She parks, and we step out onto the soft dirt.

"She's over here," Jewel says, gesturing to headstones clustered up against the fence. I see someone bending over one of the graves, pulling weeds from the dirt mound. Jewel and I follow *Káthla* over the rough ground.

As we walk up, Raymond stands, wiping dust off his hands. His face is closed like always, but I'm still glad to see him. "I'm so sorry," I say. "I never told you that before."

Raymond nods slowly, and for the first time he looks right at me and almost smiles.

Small gifts blanket Tela's grave: seashells, a worn Teddy bear, a scattering of beads. "I brought her something." I pull the pomegranate out of the paper sack and set it gently among them.

Standing between Raymond and Jewel, *Káthla* reaches into the pocket of her jacket. She puts a small buckskin bag in my hand. "This is for you."

The top is tied closed by two leather strings with gold, blue, and green beads at the ends. It smells like the campfire out on Sidwalter Butte.

My fingers feel something hard beneath the smooth, soft leather. I slowly work the bag open and pull out a small rock. It's deep red and rough, just like the earth under the junipers all across the reservation. And it feels as warm in the flat of my hand.

The sadness rises in my throat. "Tomorrow I have to go."

"You remember that day I came to your house," *Káthla* says.

It feels like a long time ago. *The animals who were people and the people who were always here.* "Yes."

Káthla looks into my eyes. "Your roots are inside you, too." She touches the bag in my hand. "Carry this to remember that they go with you always."

I look at *Káthla,* at Jewel and Raymond. In their familiar faces, I now see what I couldn't for so long. I want to fold their strength and pain and kindness into my heart, the way *Káthla* tucked this little rock into the bag. Where they will be whenever I need them.

"I won't forget you," I say, blinking back tears.

The cemetery is peaceful and quiet in the morning sun. From here, I can see far over the rolling hills of sagebrush and juniper, even farther off into the dark mountains beyond.

Something to hold in my hand. Maybe this will be enough for now. The rest I can figure out as it comes.

Acknowledgments

Thanks, first, to my parents, the real Bud and Mary Schlick, for starting this long journey. They left Iowa in 1950, a young married couple setting their sights on the West. They didn't know then that they
would spend the rest of their lives living among and working with
Indian people. I've always been grateful for the life that I was born
into. Thanks, too, to my brothers for lending so much of the best
parts of themselves to the characters of Bill and Joe.

The kids I knew at Warm Springs from 1960 to 1964 inspired
the characters that became Kitty's classmates and friends. I'm grateful to each person I know still and to those who live in my memory.
In particular, I wish to honor one courageous classmate, now gone,
who lives on in the spirit of Jewel.

In 1997, I wrote the first piece that would evolve into this book as
an exercise at Fishtrap, a writing workshop in the Wallowa Mountains of northeastern Oregon. I thank my instructor, Sandra Osawa,
and Fishtrap faculty in later workshops where more of Kitty's story
found the page: Richard Garcia, Craig Lesley, John Rember, Peter
Sears, and Kim Stafford.

Throughout this process, I've been blessed by the supportive cri-
tique of fellow writers: Katie Benmar, Mallory Clarke, Riley Fleet,
Stephanie Guerra, Coy Heaton, Damion Heintschel, Bonnie Camp-
bell Hill, Nancy J. Johnson, Bridget Turner Kelly, Erin Keogh, Frances
McCue, Margit McGuire, Claudia Mason, Maureen Massey, Steve
Milam, Megan Morrison, Di Murphy, Mark Roddy, Regie Routman,
Megan Sloan, and countless others who read and encouraged. I also
appreciate the cheerful research support of Bob Novak of the Lemieux
Library at Seattle University.

I owe more than I can say to Dinah Stevenson at Clarion and to Marjorie Naughton, who introduced us. Feedback from Marcia Leonard came at just the right time and made all the difference.

Finally, it comes back to my family, who walked every step with me: Mary Dodds Schlick, Joseph and Patty Schlick, Margarete Noe, Joseph and Jessica Noe, Jack Noe, and Russ Noe (who read every word out loud and laughed and cried in all the right places), and in their lifetimes, William T. (Bud) Schlick, Bill Schlick, and Jerre Noe.

Author's Note

Kitty's story is inspired by my own. Like Kitty, I moved to the Warm Springs Reservation in central Oregon in the early 1960s. Like her dad, mine worked for the Bureau of Indian Affairs as the forest manager. My family attended church in Madras. We swam in Shitike Creek. My brothers played baseball on the VFW Little League team, just like Bill and Joe.

We lived at Warm Springs from 1960 to 1964. My brothers and I were among seventeen non-Indian students in the school of three hundred on the reservation. Unlike Kitty, I felt welcomed and accepted by my classmates from the beginning. I experienced what Kitty's mother urges her to consider about being the new kid: "People are kind and generous here. If you give that girl a chance to know you, you'll see."

Many of Kitty's experiences at school are based on events in my real life. One of my teachers read the Bible to us every day. A boy fell through the ceiling of my fifth grade class when he was working in the attic. We cut out cardboard masks with razorblades, and, like Kitty, I cut my desk and lived in fear that I would be caught.

We also sang the Oregon state song, celebrated Columbus Day, and learned of the courage of the pioneers who followed the Oregon Trail. And I was aware, even as a ten-year-old, that my Indian classmates sometimes were treated like outsiders on their own land.

The school, now called Warm Springs Elementary, has changed a lot since Kitty, Pinky, Jewel, and Raymond would have been students. The principal is a member of the Klamath tribe. Students now learn things in school that relate to their lives on the reservation. For example, the school teaches lessons in the languages of the three tribes who live there: Ichishkiin, the language of the Warm Springs people; Kiksht, the Wasco language; and Numu, the Paiute language.

Although the characters in Kitty's life are fictional, they remind me of people I knew at Warm Springs. Today those classmates and friends are parents and grandparents, members of the tribal council, business leaders, and police officers. Pinky, the inspiration for her namesake character, remains a valued friend.

All my life, other non-Indians have asked me, "What was it like living on an Indian reservation?" I found part of an answer in Kitty's story. It applies to people no matter who we are, or where or when we live. Through her journey as a lonely girl who just wants to fit in, Kitty learns to reach out to others. With the help of caring friends, she comes to understand that belonging is something she holds always, inside her heart.

⤙⤙⤙HOH⤚⤚⤚

To learn more about the people, history, culture, and government of the reservation, visit the websites of the Confederated Tribes of Warm Springs (www.warmsprings.com) and The Museum at Warm Springs (www.museumatwarmsprings.org). My mother, Mary Dodds Schlick, told the true story of my family's life on the Colville, Warm Springs, and Yakama Reservations in her memoir, *Coming to Stay: A Columbia River Journey* (University of Washington Press, 2007).

Glossary and Pronunciation Guide

Three tribal languages are spoken on the Warm Springs Reservation: Ichishkiin (Warm Springs tribe), Kiksht (Wasco tribe), and Numu (Paiute tribe). Words that come from a specific language are identified below.

Báshtan (buhsh-tin). **Ichishkiin.** A term for non-Indians, sometimes used derogatorily; from "Boston man" to describe non-Indian explorers and traders from the east.

Celilo Falls (suh-lie-low). The largest and best known of the many traditional fishing areas on the Columbia River. Called *Wy-am* ("echo of falling water"), Celilo Falls was a major gathering and trading place for native people from throughout the Pacific Northwest and beyond. The falls were destroyed when the last gates on The Dalles Dam were closed on March 10, 1957. Within hours, the waters of the Columbia River backed up behind the dam and drowned this ancient cultural treasure.

HeHe (hee-hee). A forested butte near the highway between Warm Springs and Portland, Oregon. HeHe is the site of one of the important first-foods ceremonies, the Huckleberry Feast, held in late summer.

Káthla (kaht-la). **Ichishkiin.** "Grandmother"; specifically, "mother's mother."

Nch'i-wána (inch-ee-wanna). The Columbia River, which forms much of the border between Oregon and Washington. Also called The Big River, the Columbia has had many names through the centuries; this is the name most commonly used among the native peoples of the region.

Paiute (pie-yute). One of the three tribal groups living on the Warm Springs Reservation. In the 1870s, the U.S. Army forced the Numu-speaking Paiute people to leave their traditional lands in the desert areas of southeastern Oregon. Many came to the Warm Springs Reservation, where they were welcomed by the Warm Springs and Wasco tribes.

papoose (pa-pooss). A term for a young Indian child that comes from the Narragansett language of the 1600s. This term is not generally used by native people and is often considered to be offensive.

Queahpama (kwee-uh-pahma). A Warm Springs family name.

Sahme (sah-mee). A Warm Springs family name.

Seekseequa (seek-seek-wuh). Name of a creek and canyon at the southern end of the Warm Springs Reservation.

Shitike Creek (shih-tike). The creek and road that run past the community of Warm Springs; also Shitike Butte, on which the Shitike lookout tower stands.

Warm Springs. The tribal group for which the reservation is named. The Ichishkiin-speaking Warm Springs people traditionally fished on the Columbia River and its tributaries and also traveled across a wide territory to hunt game and gather roots and berries. The Warm Springs Reservation was established in 1855 when the U.S. government negotiated a treaty with representatives of the Wasco and Warm Springs tribes. The tribal representatives gave up nearly ten million acres of land and reserved a fraction of their original territory for their exclusive use. The treaty maintains tribal rights to fish, hunt, and gather other foods outside of the reservation.

Wasco (wahs-ko). One of the three tribal groups living on the reservation. The Kiksht-speaking Wasco people traditionally lived and fished on the Columbia River and are known for basketry with unique and intricate designs.